FUR AND FANGS

THE EVIE CHESTER FILES: CASE 3

NITA ROUND

Cover Design
MAY DAWNEY

Editorial Services
KRISTA

PINK
TEA
BOOKS

To readers everywhere

To my wife
Without her absolutely none of this would be possible

1

———

"Stuff this!" Evie Chester grumbled.

She stared at the chalkboard covered in ill-formed squiggles and dumped it on the table. Even then, the messy white marks still taunted her. This wasn't the first time she'd expressed her frustration about writing, and it wouldn't be the last. She slumped into her seat. "I'm never going to get the hang of this. I really don't know why I bother."

Hesta Bethwood sighed and glanced at Evie over the top of her newspaper. "Focus and try again. It will come. You just have to keep practicing your letters." She cocked her head to one side to read what had been written. "My something is Evie something and I was a something or other. "

"See? Useless!"

At that, Agatha Hickman, Evie's landlady entered the room. "What's wrong with Evie?"

"Getting annoyed with herself again," Hesta replied.

Evie crossed her hands over her chest. "I'm here, you know."

"We know," Hesta said, and turned back to Agatha. "She's frustrated with her lessons. Again."

"Of course, I'm frustrated. I should just give up right now and save myself the time and effort."

"Evie, dear," Agatha said, "you *must* learn how to read and write. You know you must, so you might as well buckle down and get on with it." She reached out and looked at what Evie had been working on. "Look, you should try and print the letters clearly rather than joining them in a cursive style. For now, just make sure you get the right letters in the right places and that'll be enough."

"But—" Evie started.

"No buts, just continue. You're making very good progress," Agatha said. "How are you doing on the reading?"

"Slowly," Evie admitted. "I'll never be able to—"

"Hush," Hesta interrupted. "It's only been a few weeks."

Evie shrugged and picked up the chalkboard. She wiped off what she had written and tried again.

"Have you read the papers, Agatha?" Hesta asked.

"No. Not yet. Anything of interest?"

"There's been another murder over in Cainstown. They're calling him the Butcher of Bristelle."

Agatha shook her head. "That's not unusual. Murders are plentiful in Cainstown. Why would the papers be interested in what happens to a few poor people?"

"Normally, they wouldn't," Hesta agreed, "but there are exceptional circumstances in this case."

"Such as?"

"For one, it says here that the constabulary thinks it's the work of the same killer."

"But that doesn't explain why the papers are interested," Agatha countered. "Violence is as common as horse droppings."

"They're interested because they've also found remains in Queens Park, up by Castle Hill."

"Well, now, that puts an entirely new complexion on things, doesn't it? Queens Park is too close to where the important people live. They'll not tolerate a murder on their doorstep without some outcry," Agatha said.

"Exactly so."

"Do they know who the victim is?

Hesta shook her head. "No. They say the remains are too difficult to identify, like those in Cainstown. The papers speculate whether the killer is a man or a wild beast of some sort."

Agatha snorted. "What kind of animal can hide in a city like Bristelle without being seen?"

"Only the human kind of animal, if you ask me," Hesta said. "But they probably don't want folk to panic at the thought that they don't have a clue who is up to such vile misdeeds."

"I'm not sure the idea of a wild beast that no one can find is any more comforting than an unknown person."

"True enough."

Agatha nodded her head thoughtfully. "Anyway, enough of violence and the like. Have you two decided what you're up to today?"

"I thought I would move back to Bethwood House," Hesta said.

Evie looked up from her scribbles. "Today? Why?"

"Well, I can't keep taking up your space for one thing."

"I don't mind. You don't take up too much room. But you do snore."

Hesta laughed. "Thank you. I appreciate what you have both done for me here, but I need to move on. There are affairs to be settled and many more things to do…" Her voice, and her humour, faded away. "I never thought I would be burying my brother so young. He always had such life in him."

"I'm sorry for your loss," Agatha said.

"Me too," Evie said. "Even though we didn't see eye to eye, as it were, no one deserved to die the way he did."

"Thank you. Thank you both. I'm not sure what I would have done without you."

" You never would have been alone, with all your family in the theatre. They would have been there for you," Evie said.

"Yes," Hesta agreed.

"Have you heard from the coroner?" Agatha asked.

Hesta nodded. "Finally. The authorities have stated that there is no evidence of foul play of any kind, at least not on our part."

"Was there any doubt?" Agatha asked.

"Two grown men dropping dead like that looks a little suspicious, don't you think?" Hesta asked.

"Well, yes, it would have been better if they had borne some signs of a fight. At least then the cause of death would have been plain and obvious."

"Exactly," Hesta said.

"I was thinking about those murders. Are you sure you'll be safe in your house with some crazed monster on the loose?" Agatha asked.

"I'll make sure I don't go out alone at night. I should be safe enough."

"And don't go using your skill in plain sight," Evie said. "I heard some grumbles down in the market, and it seems there is a growing fear of witches again."

"Witches, indeed," Hesta said, and shook her head.

"You should both be careful right now. I warned Florie when she set out earlier," Agatha said.

Evie chuckled. "Well, a firestarter creating flames all over the city would be a little obvious."

"She knows better than that, and they will take care of her over at the theatre," Hesta said. "And her young man, Simon, he'll look after her and make sure she doesn't do anything silly." She turned to Evie. "And that just leaves you. You'll have to be very careful when you go to the hospital. No sucking out diseases when people are watching. We don't want anyone taking you for a witch."

"What about the old wife, Oklah Wehari?" Evie asked.

"Her people will take care of her," Hesta said. "No one in Cainstown will let harm come to Oklah."

"Even though she is more of a witch than we are?"

"She's a herb woman, wise in old lore. They can accept that without fear of witchcraft. Besides, she's lived amongst the Cainstowners for years, and they know her well. Enough to think well of her and maybe even be a little protective of her."

"I hope so," Evie said.

"Anyway, I'd best get my things together," Hesta said. "Charlie is coming to fetch me in the calash. He wants me to meet his wife."

"His wife?" Agatha asked. "You're taking a social visit with your driver?"

"No, not at all. I need a housekeeper, as well as a driver and someone to take care of house maintenance. Charlie can do both of the latter things, and his wife needs a new position, so that would take care of household management. They'll have the room at the top of the house."

"Oh, that should work out very well for you," Agatha observed.

"I think so, too. I'll have people in the house to take care of things, and I won't be left alone." Hesta stood up and held out her hand to Evie. "Come help me pack my things?"

Without a second thought, Evie accepted Hesta's proffered hand. "Of course."

Upstairs in Evie's room, Hesta didn't have many things to pack. She pushed her spare clothing and personal items into a small bag. "Now you'll have your bed back to yourself," she said.

Evie shook her head. "I'll miss you."

"Even though I snore?"

"Yes, even then. It's comforting."

"My snoring is comforting?" Hesta chuckled.

"No, silly." Evie moved away and stood next to the small window that overlooked Ardmore Street.

"Evie?"

"Everything is different now, isn't it?"

Hesta joined her at the window. "It is. Not so long ago I was a Siren without a voice, and then you came along and gave my song back to me."

"Once, not so long ago, I was a slave. Then I met you, and you set me free."

"And even though you didn't trust me or my brother for the wrongs we'd done to you, you stayed."

"I know," Evie said. "But then we fought a demon together and won. Look how many people we've saved from an otherworld infestation."

"We might have saved the people of Cainstown and Bristelle, but it cost me my brother."

"I'm sorry. For all his faults, he was important to you, and I respect that."

"Now I'm all alone."

Evie turned to Hesta. "No, you're not alone, never alone. Florie worships you, and even Agatha has grown to like you. The people from the theatre adore you also. How could you ever think of yourself as alone?"

Hesta stared into her eyes. "What about you, Evie?"

"I'll always be there for you. Will you be there for me?"

"Of course I will. For one thing, we have work to do with the library and the academy."

"Of course, how silly of me to forget." Evie sighed. "You know, you could stay here a little while longer. You could sort out the practicalities of life just as well from here, and you'd have us to keep you company."

Hesta placed her hand on Evie's arm and squeezed. "Are you trying to keep me here with you?"

Evie didn't answer.

"Anyway," Hesta continued, "I have so many things to sort out, maybe you should come and stay with me instead. It's closer to the hospital, and…and then I won't be so alone."

Abruptly, Evie flung her arms around Hesta and held her tight. "You're never alone. I'm always here, and don't you forget it."

2

A little after tea time, Evie stood outside a large four-storey, red brick building at the north end of Bristelle. The hospital. She stood at the entrance under the protection of the covered portico as she gathered herself together. After a long, deep breath, she strode through the entrance into the reception foyer.

A guard at the reception desk looked up as she entered. "Can I assist you?" he asked.

"I'm here to see Doctor Joym Montgomery. He's expecting me," she replied. It sounded so strange to go through the front door and announce herself, as though she had importance of her own.

"Name, please."

"Evie Chester."

He didn't look convinced of her important at all, yet he picked up a clipboard and scanned the list. "I have you here. Please take a seat in the waiting room until the doctor is available." He pointed at one of the open doors to the side of the reception area.

She stopped just outside the door. "Here?"

He nodded. "Yes, ma'am."

Being called ma'am was even more unusual. Evie smiled to herself. It looked like she was on her way up in the world. Or at the least, she'd arrived at a level where they considered her a human being and not property. That said, with a gift like hers, there would be many, she thought, who would take advantage of her and make her gift a part of their assets.

Doctor Montgomery didn't keep her waiting long. He still wore clothing for the street rather than the wards. He stared at her for a moment, and it seemed to Evie that the good doctor had a few things going through his mind right then.

Then his light brown eyes softened.

"Come, Evie, let's talk. You have given me a few things to think about these last few days," he said. "But I think I have a solution that benefits us all."

"Doctor?"

"First, I will have you trained with the nurses so you might learn all of the basics of care in a hospital."

"But I can't—"

"Read," he finished for her. "I know. You will need to learn. However, I suggest you tell no one of your lack of ability. You are already learning, are you not?"

She nodded. "I have reading lessons every day. Two or three times a day most days."

"Good, good. There is a small group being trained by Matron Davids. I will introduce shortly. She knows that you are not able to read and write, so she will assist. Do not, under any circumstances, tell her or anyone else that you are gifted."

"Yes, doctor."

"Good, I'm glad you understand. However, when you are on rounds with me, please also be circumspect about your gift, and let's see what we can discover together."

Evie grinned. "Yes, I would like that most of all."

"Excellent. Let me show you to Matron Davids. She will want you to accompany her for an hour every morning to learn the basics with the others. After that, I would like to see you every evening for a walk through the wards. I would really appreciate your assistance with post-surgical patients."

His eyes almost glowed as he spoke; this was important to him.

"We lose a lot of patients during, and just after, surgery. The soporifics are not always reliable or safe and we lose far too many due to using ether or chloroform. Why that happens, we don't know, and the reasons may remain one of the great mysteries of medicine that we'll never understand." He stared at her as though to make sure she followed him.

"It's a risky business," Evie said.

"Indeed. Afterwards, the trauma of surgery takes a toll, and some fail to last more than a day. Even if they last beyond the first few days, then we have to contend with infections."

"I am sure you all do everything you can."

He sighed. "Never mind, that is a discussion for another day. And soon you will understand the reasons why some things work and some things don't. First, let's get you settled, shall we?"

"Yes, doctor, of course."

"This way. The staff room is where I shall introduce you to the matron. She's expecting us."

Matron Davids wore a burgundy uniform with a burgundy colored head wrap around her grey hair. Her light brown skin did not show much in the way of wrinkles, and she stood with her shoulders back and stiff.

"Evie Chester, I presume?" she asked. Her light brown eyes, flecked with green, stared into Evie, as though she could see inside her mind.

Evie nodded.

"You are a little old to start nursing, but I'll have you caught up before you know it."

"Yes, matron."

Davids smiled. "And polite, too. Listen closely, do as you are told, and we will get on well enough."

"Of course, Matron Davids."

"First, you need a uniform." Davids opened a cupboard with a key that hung from her belt. She pulled out a uniform and head wrap. "Change into this uniform. At the end of your shift, put the soiled clothing into the basket in the corner. You can get a fresh set every time you come into work."

"Thank you. Should I go and get changed now, matron? Is there someplace private I can go?"

Davids looked at Doctor Montgomery. "Doctor, do you have any further instructions?"

"Indeed. Prepare as usual, show her around, and get her started on the basics for the wards. Then bring her to me." He looked at his timepiece. "Say in about an hour, in the post-surgical wards."

"Doctor, is it not a little premature to take a new girl onto the complex wards?"

"Normally I would say so, but our Evie is a very talented young woman, and I promised that I would give her the tour."

Matron stared at Evie thoughtfully. "Well, let's see what this one has to offer. In an hour it is, doctor."

"Thank you." He turned away and left them to it.

"Best rush and change then, Miss Evie Chester," Davids said. She pointed to a door. "Change in there."

"Yes, matron," Evie said.

She followed Matron Davids into the next room. The tiled walls and floor marked it as a washing area. There were signs on the walls, too, but Evie, of course, had no idea what they said.

At the far end of the room were a number of partitioned areas. Davids handed her a uniform. "Change in one of those cubicles and pull the curtains closed."

The curtains went almost all the way across, but that didn't worry Evie. There was no one about other than the matron. She removed her clothes as fast as she could so she could dress in the generous uniform.

"You'll need a belt for that, but let's see how you do today. This is the nurses' area, and the signs tell you what you must do," Davids said.

Evie was about to remind her that she couldn't read when Davids pointed to each of the signs. "This one says that all nurses must be showered and clean before work commences. Come in an hour before your duty starts and wash thoroughly. We do not want our patients infected with the filth of the world outside."

Evie nodded.

"The other signs are reminders about cleanliness, and one, as you can see, contains instructions on how to wash your hands. Let me demonstrate." Davids used her forearm to knock a brass lever to the side, and water gushed into a large, deep basin. She let the water run until it grew hot enough that steam rose up and clouded the mirror over the sink.

"Wash your hands under hot water. It won't get hot enough to scald, but the hotter the better. Use the soap provided, and when you start, nudge this other lever to the side. Never use your hands on a lever, always use your arm. Like this." Davids nudged the lever with her arm, and the *click click* of the ratchet mechanism ended with a louder *clunk.* Davids stopped pushing the lever and started to wash her hands. A loud *tick tock,* louder even than the *whoosh* of the tap water, echoed in the empty room. "Now you scrub," she said, and used the soap and a hard brush to wash her hands and arms up to the elbow. "Don't skimp on the soap, and make sure you scrub your nails, too."

Evie nodded, although Davids was focused on washing her hands rather than anywhere else.

After several minutes of washing, a *ting* announced the

end of the wash cycle. Davids turned the water lever off with her elbow and shook off the surplus water.

"My hands are clean, but they will not stay clean if I leave them wet or damp." She took a small linen cloth from a pile of similar cloths, dried her hands, and threw the used cloth into a wash basket.

Evie tried to use her gift to look at Davids' hands, but she was not always good at detecting anything unnatural when it was out in the air.

"Now you do it," Davids instructed. "As you can't be reminded by signs, I have to hope you have a good memory."

"Yes, matron," Evie replied. She performed the routine she'd just watched, and exactly so. If anything, she brushed at her hands a little more vigorously.

"Cleanliness is the most important thing in this hospital. We have standards. Most of all, we have the lowest rate of infection in all of the Angles, possibly in most of the world. We'd like to continue our good standing." When Evie had finished, the matron said, "Show me your hands." She nodded as she examined Evie's palms, and then her nails. "Excellent. Please make sure you continue exactly this way."

"Yes, matron."

Davids smiled. "I had my doubts about you, but I think we'll get on splendidly. I'll show you around, get you accustomed to our ways, and then I'll take you to the doctor."

"Thank you, matron."

3

E vie found Doctor Montgomery as he was leaving the post-surgery ward. "Miss Chester, how has your evening been so far?" he asked.

"Good. Matron Davids has been most instructive and helpful."

"Good, good. Your timing is perfect. All the other medics and nurses have things to do in the wards, and I'm checking things as I end my day. It is a quiet time for me, and I get a chance to look at the areas that most appeal."

"Post-surgical infections and diseases."

"Just so."

"And also where I might be of most use to you."

He nodded. "I would like to understand how your gift works."

"Me too," she answered.

"You don't know?"

"No. I hope this is going to help me understand it better."

He nodded. "Let me take you to see a patient who has a fever. A fever is indicative of an infection. Other symptoms allow you to determine what kind of infection it is."

"So all infections are different?"

He smiled. "We think so, but it is so hard to find them when they are so small."

"How does the hand cleaning help?"

The doctor waved his hands about. "There are little organisms everywhere, and if we have too many, they make us sick."

Evie thought about that for a moment. "So why can't I see the sickness in the air like I can see demons?"

"Well, demons, I think, have no place in this world, which makes them unnatural and evil. Life, natural life, no matter how small it is, has a place here. They live and they die just as we do. Some of them find their way into the wrong place and there is a fight for control. That is what makes us sick."

"But that doesn't…" Evie didn't finish her sentence. The doctor didn't interrupt her either as she began to piece together information and experience. "I thought it was about naturalness for a moment, but perhaps it's about ownership."

"And the fight in the body," he added.

She nodded. She needed to think more about this. "Shall we see this feverish patient of yours?"

"Come this way." He led her to a bed in the middle of the ward and drew the isolating curtains around the bay. The man on the bed lay asleep on his back. He looked peaceful, although sweat gathered in small drops around his hair line, and at the side of his head he had perspired so much that his hair clung damply to his skin.

At the foot of the metal bed frame hung a clipboard that the doctor looked at. "This is Michael Witham. He came in with a low-grade fever, which has grown worse since his arrival. He is responding to medication, but not as fast as we would have expected."

"Has he awoken?" Evie asked.

"Yes, but he is always exhausted and sleeps easily."

Evie called her gift so she could look at Michael more closely. At this point, she didn't touch him; this was not about curing, but about understanding. She saw several areas she presumed were the cause of the problem. An abdominal area flared and pulsed with infection. But she knew there was more to the problem than what she first saw.

"What can you see?" he asked her.

"Will you tell me what is wrong with him?"

"After you tell me what you see."

A test, Evie thought, but testing her was better than dismissing her. She examined the patient from head to foot. "Anything else? Any pains?"

"A headache, which often accompanies a high fever. He also complained of a backache, but that's probably because he works at the slaughterhouse by the docks and lifts heavy carcasses."

"Oh, right." She focused her attention on his back, but it was hard to see what was there. "Can I look at the skin and touch him?"

"You're clean and have exercised the proscribed hand hygiene?"

"Of course," she replied.

"Then do as you feel necessary."

She pulled back the covers and opened the man's shirt. A piece of gauze covered a section of his side. She removed the dressing and looked at the raw wound underneath. It oozed blood and infection in spite of the dressing and antiseptics.

"Straight to business, then?"

She ignored him and prodded the patient's ribs. Then she looked at his knees and prodded there, too. Using her gift only to look took more effort, as though it was not the primary purpose of her gift. She filed that information for later consideration.

"It's not his legs that are the problem, Miss Chester," the doctor said.

She moved towards Michael's head. She saw inflammation along the back of his neck just as there had been along the edge of his ribs. She touched the back of his neck and her gift sampled the nature of this flaring. Her mouth filled with the taste of wet and moldy hay.

She stood back from the bed and let her thoughts settle.

"I think he has mid-sea fever, or the Goatman's Gift. I've seen this before."

The doctor stared at her for a moment. "You don't think the wound in his side is the cause of his problems?"

Evie shrugged. "It's important, but it is not the whole story," she said. Couldn't he see that? But then it occurred to her. He didn't have her skills; he was essentially a blind man trying to see what he never could. She realized then the advantages she had—not only could she examine the visible symptoms in more depth than available to the naked eye, but she could also see and detect things others could not. Her assistance would be invaluable.

"Wounds never help, of course. They sap his strength and when he is laid so low, more infections can take advantage. Even so, I think the main sickness is the mid-sea fever."

He shook his head. "We don't get mid-sea fever in Bristelle. It is mostly caught by herders, which is why they call it Goatman's Gift. There are no goat herders in or near the city."

"Yes, but you said he works in a slaughterhouse?" Evie asked. She knew what she saw. "Isn't that a place to catch it, too?"

He stroked his chin and looked thoughtful, but said no more.

"Let's fix this wound first, shall we?" Evie suggested. She'd never really thought about localized healing before, but she was determined to try anyway. As she sucked in the infection from the wound, she tasted rotting meat with an undertone of wet hay. "This is the infection site, after all. It feels and tastes different. I bet he cut himself with tools from work and failed to clean out the wound. He probably didn't think about it for the next few days and then the fever started."

The doctor looked at the patient's notes.

"Does it say anything about the smell when he arrived? Like wet hay?"

"Dammit," the doctor said. "Stinking clothes is all I have written here, and he was bathed and disinfected."

"Well, a slaughter man is not the best dresser nor the finest gent," she said.

"Indeed." He looked at the wound and nodded. "This looks better, and it is starting to recover already. The skin is turning pink rather than that angry red-purple. Make a mental note of this change in the skin as an indication of improving health, Miss Chester."

"Yes, doctor." She didn't mention that she had done this before, and she had a fair idea of the signs to look out for.

He examined the patient for his own benefit and made a note on the patient sheet.

"Do you want me to heal the other fever?"

He thought for a moment, and from that pause, Evie knew what he wanted.

"You want to see the progression of the other disease, don't you?"

"It would be an invaluable lesson. I have not seen Goatman's before," he admitted. "I have read of it, of course, but that isn't the same as seeing it for real."

She looked the patient over and decided he didn't look as bad as he had. She knew he wasn't in any immediate danger now that the wound had been healed, but mid-sea fever wouldn't heal itself. "I'm due in first thing tomorrow, so I can come and help out after my duties."

"What shift are you on?" he asked.

"I start at six o'clock in the morning."

"Excellent. I have until lunch tomorrow, then, to observe this illness and increase my understanding."

"And to see if I'm right or not?"

"That as well." He smiled. "Though I would like to know how you knew to look beyond the wound."

"The infections were a little different. It seemed to me that the infection from the angry-looking wound had started to seep into his blood, and I could see it running through him. Faint, but there."

The doctor nodded.

"But there were problems at the joints, too. When you said he had a backache, I saw inflammation, faint and indistinct, at the ribs and a little along the spine. It was stronger in the neck, though, and I sampled the illness."

"And what did that tell you?"

"I could taste moldy hay, I think. I've seen that before with a lad who worked with goats."

"Goats in Bristelle?"

She shook her head. "No, it was on one of the islands off Iberica."

"The islands, Evie?"

"Yes, I was there for a short while before I came to Bristelle." She hoped he wouldn't ask her any more about that.

"Right. Of course that would make sense—the islands are known for their goats, of course." The doctor stroked his chin thoughtfully. "You're quite an analyst. I'm looking forward to seeing more."

"Perhaps you could show me some other sick people. I need to learn as much as I can, and I don't mind helping."

"No curing, Evie," he whispered. "Make them a little better, no more than that. If there are too many miraculous cures, the authorities will think it a little odd and we'll get more attention than we need. I'd rather people didn't look for the gifted and witches here."

"Me either," she answered. "Maybe I should be involved a

little earlier in the process, before they display the worst of it?"

"Such as?"

Evie thought for a moment. "Perhaps I could attend a couple of surgeries to see if I can determine where the infection starts. Maybe that would allow us a chance to control the infection using ordinary measures."

"That's a little…" he started. "No, you may be onto something there. Maybe some problems start where we do not expect." He nodded, more to himself than to Evie. "We'll have to look into that a little more. Thank you for the suggestion."

"As you will, doctor."

4

———

Just outside the hospital entrance, Hesta sat in the calash and pulled the travel blanket around her knees. It had been a cold day, and at this time of night, the temperature had plummeted even further. Her hands were so cold her hands ached even though she wore gloves. The thought of a hot cup of tea grew ever more appealing.

"Miss Bethwood," Charlie said from the driver's seat, "it is very late. Are you sure Miss Chester will be here?"

"Yes," she answered. "I understand that Doctor Montgomery generally leaves the hospital in time to catch the last drink over at the Rose and Crown just off Elluth Street. I always like to know what's going on when it's important to know."

"Might I ask if that is because of Miss Chester?"

"In other circles, that could be seen as a most presumptuous observation."

"Yes, miss, but as I am now a part of your household, me and the wife also need to know what is most important in order to best assist you. And it seems to me that Miss Chester has become very significant to the Bethwood household."

"Then consider the care and consideration of Miss Chester

of vital importance. As though she's a member of the family, if you will."

"Understood. I'll let the wife know."

They remained in the shadows of the parking area for a good long while. Carriages came and went, but at this hour they were few and far between.

It was a little before the midnight hour when Hesta spotted a small, hunched figure leaving the front exit.

Evie.

She'd know her figure anywhere. Lights from the front door illuminated the small woman, and there was no mistaking the blonde and distinctive hair.

"Charlie, there she is."

"Yes, ma'am," he said. The calash surged forward as the horse responded to Charlie's command.

They drew up under the portico, but Evie was huddled in her coat and didn't appear to notice their presence.

"Hey there," Hesta called out.

Evie looked up, confusion on her face. Then she recognised them and smiled one of those rare smiles of hers that lit up her face and made her eyes twinkle.

"Hesta, what are you doing here at this hour?" she asked. Her smile vanished, replaced with a look of concern.

"You don't think I'd let you walk around the city alone at night do you?"

"I never expected you to come here."

"I know you didn't. I wanted to make sure you were safe." Hesta threw open the carriage door. "I can't have you out alone when no one knows who is safe."

Evie hauled herself into the carriage. "Thank you," she said. She closed her eyes and with a heartfelt sigh of relief slumped in the seat.

Hesta looked at Evie's face and noted the dark circles under her eyes.

"You look exhausted, was it a hard evening?"

"Yes," Evie replied.

"Did you do your thing?" Hesta asked.

"Some, yes, and now I'm completely wiped out."

"Did you purge?"

Evie's eyes flew open. "No. I forgot, and I've held some for a few hours now."

"Charlie, get us to Bethwood House as quick as you can." She grabbed Evie's hand. "It's all right, you'll be safe at my house."

"Don't touch me, I might… I'm not sure I can stop myself," Evie said. She tried to pull away, but Hesta didn't let her.

"You won't hurt me, Evie. I don't think you would allow it."

"This is not the time to test your theories," Evie said, but she smiled nonetheless.

Hesta pushed strands of hair from Evie's face. "Your hair is wet. Are you getting a temperature?" She held the back of her hand against Evie's head.

"No, I had a shower after the shift. You know I never catch anything, but I don't want to take any sickness from the hospital into the city. I must do the same as everyone else." Evie looked into Hesta's eyes. "I must be a perfect student, and be exactly as they expect."

"I understand." She didn't release Evie's hand though, not until they pulled up outside Bethwood House.

"Charlie, I'm finished for the night. Evie will stay here in case she is unwell."

"Right you are," he said. "I'll get the missus to make sure the guest room is set up, and we'll make a pot of something hot."

"Excellent idea, thank you," Hesta said. She had to help Evie out of the carriage; it seemed that she wilted a bit more with every passing minute. "Come on, let's get you inside."

"I really need to purge."

"I know, my sweet. Let's get you to some place private." She led Evie around the side of the house.

They were almost to the back door when Evie said, "Stop."

Hesta let go of Evie and stepped back. Evie's purge was not a pleasant thing to watch. She'd seen it a few times, and even now, she didn't know whether to be fascinated or horrified. She'd seen the many different colours of the vile things Evie had absorbed and then shed. In the darkness at the side of the house, it all looked dark, like oil. Or blood. She wanted to reach out and help, but she knew this was something Evie had to do alone.

When Evie retched and heaved against the wall, Hesta couldn't stop herself. She reached out and stroked her back. "Let it out. It's fine," she soothed. The stench of the excretion from her fingers, eyes, and mouth almost made Hesta retch alongside Evie. But she didn't. She would be strong for Evie; she couldn't leave her to suffer alone. If it was bad enough to see and smell, what was it like to be the one ridding herself of this disagreeable vileness?

"I'm done," Evie said. "I'm tired. I'm not normally this tired."

"Maybe you kept it inside too long? Anyway you probably need something to eat and drink. When was the last time you ate?"

Evie shrugged. "Earlier."

"Come in. Tea should be ready by now, and I think we'll add a little honey. That should help you."

They made it inside to the drawing room, where a fire already blazed in the grate. Warmth filled the room and almost the moment Hesta got Evie onto the couch, Mrs. Dunn brought tea.

"Thank you, Mrs. Dunn," Hesta said.

"Is the little one all right?"

"I'm fine," Evie said as she struggled to sit up.

"Mrs. Dunn, this is Evie Chester."

"Of course. The guest room will be ready in a few moments," she said.

"Thank you. I appreciate your help. After that, you should get some sleep. It's late. I'm sorry to keep you up so long. Charlie, too," Hesta said.

"We're happy to help, Miss Bethwood. Will you two be all right?"

"We'll be fine, thank you. Good night."

"Good night, Miss Bethwood, Miss Chester." The door closed behind her, and the latched closed with a quiet click.

"Mrs. Dunn?" Evie asked.

"Charlie and his wife help out around the house now. It's a new arrangement, of course, but it seems to be working well so far."

"Oh, yes, you mentioned something at Agatha's house. I forgot."

"Never mind the household arrangements. I'm not sure you should be out so late at night. Not alone," Hesta said.

"I'm fine. I can manage. I always manage."

"I didn't say you couldn't. Did you not hear the whistles?"

"Whistles? What whistles?" Evie asked.

"The constabulary whistles. There was another killing this evening, Evie. I don't think it's safe for you to walk home late at night. I don't think it's safe for you to walk anywhere at any time. Besides, it's a long way from the hospital to Ardmore." She shook her head. "No, there is no way I'd let you walk all that way alone. I had to make sure you were safe."

Evie didn't reply. If anything, she looked shocked, and for a moment, Hesta thought she might cry.

"Are you all right?"

Evie nodded. "No one, other than Florie and Agatha, has ever been interested in my safety before. And even their concern is not like this."

"I've told you how important you are to me."

Evie leaned back against the couch and smiled. "People say one thing and mean another all the time."

"I don't. I'm not like other people." *Especially where you are concerned*, she wanted to add, but she couldn't say that. She wasn't sure what Evie wanted, and she didn't want to impose on Evie any more than necessary.

"Hesta," Evie said, "you're important to me, too."

5

E vie arrived early to her shift. She used the showers
before any of the nurses arrived, and found a uniform
heavy with starch for herself. It rustled when she walked, and
the stiffness at the collar irritated her neck. She began the
process of washing her hands as she had done the night
before, and although she was tired, her good mood gave her a
boost of energy.

Matron Davids entered the washroom at the same time as
a half dozen other women. "Well, Evie Chester. Prompt and
efficient, I see."

"Yes, matron," she replied.

Davids clapped her hands together. "Hurry up, girls. This
is Evie Chester. She's new, but unlike you lot, she's prompt
and efficient."

The other girls glared at her.

"Get washed. Get dressed. Clean your hands, and I'll meet
you in the staff room," Davids continued. "Evie, come
with me."

They sat down on two of the chairs in the staff room, and
Davids stared at her as though she had something unpleasant
to say.

"Yes, matron, is there a problem?" Evie asked.

Davids straightened her skirt and stared at her for a few moments. "This is technically your first day. You've had no chance to be introduced to the wards in the same way as the other young women, and there are a great many things that you will have to learn to catch up to them."

"Yes, matron."

"But I know you have spent time with Doctor Montgomery. No doubt you've acquired more knowledge from him than most would, and you are more mature than the others, so perhaps this is not such an issue."

Evie nodded.

"Today's lesson plan includes a mortuary visit. If the girls can't cope with dead bodies, then there is no room for them in a hospital." She paused as though she expected Evie to say something or react a little. Evie kept her face blank and did not react. "Also, today we have been invited to a dissection in the Rotunda. Do you know where that is?"

"Yes, matron. I've attended a demonstration there."

"What? How did you manage that?"

"I was the guest of Godwyn and Hesta Bethwood at the demonstration of mesmerism and animal magnetism."

"Were you indeed. Did you also observe the near-riot they had?"

"We did, yes. We were in the middle of it, and it was a most unpleasant and scary experience," Evie said.

"Then what about a dissection? It's a most upsetting process, if you're at all squeamish."

"Squeamish? Not in the slightest."

Davids stared at her.

"At least I don't think so," Evie said.

Davids nodded at Evie's uncertainty. "Then we shall see your reaction during the demonstration."

"Yes, matron."

"I'll make sure you sit closest to the demonstration," Davids said.

The door swung open from the washing area, and the others in her group came into the staff room. "Ladies, I'm so glad you could join us. Brief introductions, then. This is Evie Chester. She has just joined the group. Please extend to her the greatest courtesy." She pointed to each of the nurses-in-training in turn "This is Jenee, Frannie, Minnie, Betty, and Suzan."

"Hello," they said, almost in unison.

Evie tried to smile. "Hello."

"Now, as you would have been told, today is a morning of death. The mortuary calls us." Davids stood up. "This way, please, and don't dawdle."

The women groaned quietly as Davids left the room, but if the matron heard them, she gave no indication. One by one they followed Davids into the corridor. She marched them across the hospital ground floor and led them down the steps into the basement. The lower level looked like all the other floors in the building except here white tiles covered every floor and wall. Because there were no windows to let in any natural light, the wall lights were powered by electrics, filling the space with a yellow glow.

Davids stopped outside a pair of swing doors. She pointed to the sign and said, "This is the mortuary. Every time you fail to do your job, chances are the patient will end up here. So buck up, ladies—here is where you see the consequences of laziness, a lack of cleanliness, and other forms of incompetence."

As far as Evie knew, not all instances of death were due to nursing incompetence. Doctors, medics, surgeons, and sheer bad luck were as much to blame.

"Are we ready for what lies beyond?"

"Yes, matron," Evie said before she realized she was the only person to answer. She looked around; one of the young women grinned at her, one frowned, and the others paid her no attention. Evie didn't care much.

Davids spun on her heel and pushed through the doors. Cool air blasted out in an effort to escape someplace warmer. Evie shivered as she approached and she caught the door before it hit her in the face. She stood to the side, holding one of the doors open for the others. Not to be polite, but so no one stood behind her.

Their footsteps echoed through the vastness of the mortuary. Vaulted arches supported the roof, and between some of the arches were walled sections that rose only three quarters of the height of the room. Above these short walls, a dark space cast a gloom of such depth that the numerous lights struggled to dispel it.

Along two of the nearest walls, there were small metal doors set into the walls. They were like cupboard doors, Evie supposed, only with heavy metal levers. As the nurses walked through the room, Evie noticed the central area had more of those storage doors. Most of them had labels on them, but she couldn't get close enough to read them, even if she could understand what they said.

Davids led them to one of the doors on the side wall. The women crowded around as she opened one of the unlabeled doors. Cold rolled out of the cabinet, but the interior was too deep and dark to see much. The matron pulled out a long tray that slid smoothly on well-kept runners. As she drew the tray further out, legs sprang down.

"This is a body drawer, which is empty at this moment," she said. "The deceased are placed on one of these trays and kept inside the refrigerated drawer while they wait for either pathological examination or autopsy. They stay here until they are taken for funerary purposes."

She closed the drawer with a thud and closed the lever. "If you open a door, always be certain to close it properly with the lever in an upright position. If you don't, the refrigeration is insufficient, and the body speeds up decomposition. If anyone is caught failing to operate the doors correctly, then we'll see how you fare cleaning up such a body." The matron paused and her gaze moved from one nurse to the next, but although Evie noted a few green faces at the thought, no one flinched. Davids nodded in satisfaction. "Are you ready to see one of the cabinets that is use?"

"Yes, matron," they all answered in unison.

Davids moved along the drawers and checked the labels. "This one will do," she said. "The labels here indicate the name of the occupant and any notes that might be deemed useful. Here we have a Mr Ivan Kowsky. Found dead in his bed by his wife. Coroner reports natural causes, and he awaits transit to the funeral home." She pulled down the lever and opened the door. As before, the tray slid out without too much effort and on it a body lay covered in a plain white sheet. Nothing could be seen, yet one of the girls started to retch.

"Betty, get out. Go to the changing room and wait there. I will be with you shortly."

Betty raced from the room. The doors swung closed behind her.

Davids grabbed the ends of the sheet. "Anyone else? You'd better go now." She folded back the sheet to show the deceased man's face. "Notice the pallor of the skin, which is only noticeable in those of pale skin, like this gentleman. The color marks the first stage of death where the capillaries, the smallest of the blood vessels, have begun to close down."

She rolled the sheet to below Mr Kowsky's neck. "If you touch the skin, you'll find it cool. This is the second stage of death." She looked up at her students. "Touch him, if you want to understand the process."

Evie stepped forward and laid the back of her hand on the man's neck. It was cold and unpleasant. She managed to keep her face blank though. "Does the temperature of the body drop like this naturally, before he's stored in a refrigeration unit?"

"Can anyone tell Evie the answer?" Davids asked. No one spoke. "The answer is yes, the body loses heat until it is the same as the air temperature, then we chill further in one of these units."

Evie nodded. "Thank you."

Davids looked at the women before her. "Does anyone else want to touch?" None of the other student nurses approached.

Davids shook her head and folded the sheet further, so they could see the black stitches that stood stark against the paleness of the dead man's skin. "This is the start of the Y-incision, as the medics call it."

Evie leaned in to take a better look. "Fascinating. Why do they cut him open? Why like that? Why sew him back up afterwards now he's dead?"

"Can anyone answer that question?" Davids asked.

The others had stepped backwards, not closer, and none could answer.

"Now, ladies, don't be silly. I know none of you is squeamish." She faced the group. "Well?"

"It's spooky dealing with the dead," Minnie answered.

Davids nodded. "Very well, if you think it's too spooky, too odd, or not to your taste, then leave. Join Betty in the changing rooms. Thank you."

Evie didn't pay any attention to the girls or whether they left or not. But when she looked up, only the smiler and one other remained.

"Jenee and the ever smiling Frannie, good. I thought you two would be steadfast," Davids said. "In answer to Evie's questions, we look inside because it helps us understand the body and sickness better. Wherever possible, pathologists, who are specialist medics, dissect and conduct autopsies in order to learn what they can. This particular incision pattern is the most efficient way to get at the internal organs, and we sew him back up to make the funeral process more palatable to the grieving family."

"And this discoloring at the shoulders?"

Davids moved next to Evie and pointed to the purple discoloration underneath the shoulders. She lifted the body a little to make the marks easier to see. "This is livor mortis, the fourth stage of death, where the blood settles. It starts shortly after death and continues until full lividity is reached about eight to twelve hours later."

"Matron, you didn't mention the third stage," Frannie said.

"Correct," Davids said. "The third stage is rigor mortis, but this has already passed. I'll find an example, if you require it?"

"I've seen it," Evie said.

"Jenee and I have also," Frannie answered.

"Good. After these stages, we come to the putrefaction stages, but by then it is too late for us, unless you specialize in the mortuary. Anyway—" She began, but was interrupted when a man in black overalls crashed through the doors with a wheeled stretcher in front of him, the body on it covered by a blood-spattered sheet.

He stopped when he saw the group. "Excuse me. I didn't expect anyone to be here."

"It's all right, don't mind us. We were almost done." The matron looked thoughtful. "Who are you bringing in? It would be good for the girls to experience a more recent addition to the mortuary."

He coughed into his hand. "Begging your pardon, matron, but this one is from last night and is not really in a fit state for examination by ladies."

"Nonsense," Davids said. "A fresh one is exactly what we want and need." She brought up the sheet and covered Mr

Kowsky before she pushed him back into the drawer. The lever rose up and locked with a definite click.

Davids marched to the gurney and scanned the mound.

"Is this the beast attack?" she asked.

"Yes, matron," he answered.

"Right. Ladies, this is an opportunity few will ever get. Look at this so you might understand the nature of animal injuries." She pulled back the sheet and froze.

Whoever he'd been, he'd been severely mauled to say the least, Evie thought. There were a few things that didn't make sense to her. The blood looked a little too red, and a couple of drops spilled to the floor.

"This man didn't die last night, surely?" Davids asked.

"Yep. He was brought in by the constabulary but didn't survive long. They've tried to identify the poor bugger—"

"Language, George," Davids admonished.

"Yes, matron, but now I need to clean him up ready for autopsy," George the porter said.

Whilst they spoke, Evie noticed a couple of other things. He was a pale-skinned man, but without the pallor of death. She could see no livor mortis, and if he'd died the previous night, then she would have expected some evidence of the lividity she'd just witnessed on Mr Kowsky. Something did not measure up.

"There is definitely something wrong with this corpse," she said. Her gift rose up like a tide and filled her with a sense of foreboding unlike any other occasion.

"What?" Davids asked.

"The stages are wrong," Evie said. "Pallor is hard to see, if it exists at all, but the blood looks a little too red to me." She touched the victim's hand, but for no more than a second. "Cool. More like air temperature rather than him being as cold as Mr Kowsky." She used the edge of the sheet to lift the man's bloody hand, and then let it go and watched as it fell limply onto the gurney. "Last night?" she asked.

"There's no sign of rigor," Davids said. She looked horrified. "How about livor mortis?"

Evie used the sheet again to lift the man's shoulders. "I can't see an sign of that either."

"Good grief," Davids said. "Bodies do not fail the order of death. Is he actually dead?"

"Yes matron," George said. "They tested 'im."

"Then perhaps he has some infection that interferes with the natural orders. Isolate the body and sanitize everything and everyone until we can be examined."

Evie agreed. She'd noted something else, too. There were weak pinpricks of a shadowy luminescence that flashed darkly and died as quickly as she saw them. She'd never seen anything like it—not since she'd looked at Hesta's neck.

Hesta's neck. A curse was at work here.

She took a step backwards. "I think we need to not be anywhere near this one until we're pronounced safe," she said. "But we should get out of here and away from him."

"Evie Chester, I thought you were neither squeamish nor scared of such things."

"No matron, but—"

"Anyway it is a good idea," Davids interrupted. "Ladies, let us leave here and clean ourselves up." She turned to Evie. "Did you touch the body?"

"Yes, matron, briefly."

"Then you must stay with the mortuary porter. There are washing facilities in the back room, are there not?"

"Yes, matron," the porter answered.

"I suggest you put the body somewhere safe, and both of you scrub away any potential contamination as though your life depended on it."

"Yes, matron," Evie said."

"Until we know what this oddness is all about, take every precaution."

"Yes, matron," Evie and the porter said at the same time.

6

Evie and George wheeled the gurney into one of the autopsy rooms. It was unlocked, as nothing was left in the room when it wasn't used. Although they didn't have the keys to lock it, Evie grabbed a nearby broom and shoved the stick between the door handles.

"That won't stop anyone," George said.

"No, it won't, but they might stop and think about going inside whilst we get cleaned up," she answered.

"Right."

"I'm Evie, what's your name?" she asked. "I think Matron Davids called you George?"

"That's right," he replied.

"Well, George, let's go get changed, shall we?"

"There's only one washroom," he said. He looked at his hands and twisted his fingers together.

"Then you go first. Be thorough though. Very thorough."

He nodded. "I will, but that means you're on your own till I get back."

"Yeah, I know. I'll be fine. I'll make sure the door is safe until we can get a doctor to check things. It's probably nothing, you know, but best to be sure and careful."

He nodded enthusiastically. "Hope you're right."

"Of course I am. Now scoot, get clean. You'll need fresh clothes, too."

"Aye, I best do that." He stopped as he turned away. "Are you sure you'll be all right?"

"Of course I'll be fine. Thank you. Now go."

George strode to a doorway opposite the autopsy rooms. He paused , then slipped inside the washroom.

Evie waited for a moment or two in case he came out, then she slid the broom from out of the door handles and slipped inside the autopsy room. She half expected the body to have moved. It hadn't, but when she pulled the sheet away, the corpse glittered most darkly to her gift-assisted senses.

She stared at the glowing body but knew she would have to do something soon or leave before anyone found her in the room. Evie took a deep breath and laid her hand on the victim's shoulder. The darkness ignored her. That was new.

She could see, or rather sense through her gift, that the curse did not belong there. She could see it as it died away a bit at a time. Every flash of dark light marked the diminishment of the curse, flash by miniscule flash. Yet it appeared as though the curse fought hard to remain, regardless of the death of the host.

"What the hell are you?" she asked the body. But it didn't respond, and neither did the curse.

She stepped around the gurney and pressed the tip of her finger against an unmarked and blood-free section of skin. She was not squeamish, but she had a healthy fear of that which she did not understand. Even with her ability, nothing more revealed itself to her.

She circled the body again, searching for some clue. Anything would have helped. Yet she learned nothing more than what she had determined in the first few seconds of her examination. She touched the blood with the tip of her finger. Emotion roared into her mind, and it tasted of pure rage.

Fight. Fight. Pain.

An echo of that pain stabbed into her shoulders and ripped across her chest with such force she thought herself shredded from shoulder to gut.

Rip. Rend.

She stepped back so fast she bumped against the wall. Even then, she could hear the voice inside her head.

Kill.

The voice went silent, but her thudding heart didn't slow. She waited for a few moments before she approached the body again. She needed to know what this curse was before others suffered.

Evie found the wound that went from shoulder to gut. Long, ragged slashes, four of them, cut deep into the skin. She scrutinized the edges of the wound and for a moment, she could almost see the blood seeping from the depths of the gash.

"Not possible," she mumbled. She checked the artery in the man's neck. No pulse. She hadn't expected one since most of his chest lay open. She took one deep breath and stuck her fingers deep into the wound where the dark sparkles were most concentrated.

As blood coated her fingers, a howl like death itself filled her thoughts. She jumped back so fast she slipped and fell on her arse. It hurt. Yet the ordinary pain was normal and safe. Most of all, it took away the strange sounds inside her mind.

Whoever created this curse, she thought, they were completely insane. She cocked her head to the side as though that would help her hear the voices in her head better. She heard and felt a rage so great that no rational person could exist under the weight of all that anger. Hatred too, she decided.

A bang outside the door made Evie jump. She raced into the corridor and pushed the broom through the doors handles once more. Doctor Montgomery and Matron Davids strode into the mortuary area with a dozen porters behind them. All of them wore rubber boots, waxed coveralls, and gloves.

"Evie Chester, have you not washed yourself down yet?" Davids asked. She sounded so stern.

"I had to wait my turn. George is in the washroom," she answered. "He shouldn't be much longer."

"No time," the doctor said. "I'm sorry, Evie, trust me; this is very necessary." He waved to the porters behind him. Until then, she'd not noticed that they carried a great long pipe rolled onto a big wheel. They unraveled the pipe and, after a shout of "Now," water gushed out the end. It took two porters to hold the nozzle and another to keep the hose unkinked.

"What's that for?" Evie asked.

"Cleansing," the doctor answered.

"Now stand in the corner," Davids instructed.

Before Evie could take two steps, they turned the hose on her. A jet of ice cold water pummeled her body with such force, she thudded against the wall and dropped to the floor. She screamed and water filled her mouth.

Evie rolled into a ball to protect herself, but she couldn't escape the force of the watery blast. She thought she would drown in it. Or break in two. It was worse than being beaten by fist or boot, and felt more like being struck by a hard and unyielding iron bar.

Hesta!' she shrieked inside her thoughts, her cry for help as instinctive as making herself as small as possible.

The jet moved away, and Evie lay on the ground, her breaths coming in erratic gulps. Coldness seeped through her limbs with such overwhelming iciness that she lost sensation in her hands and feet. She struggled to her knees, but the wet tiles were too slippery to gain any kind of purchase and she slipped again.

"I don't need this," she cried out. "Please stop!"

Either they ignored her pleas, or didn't hear, a porter doused her in disinfectant, or something that smelled like it. Evie scrunched her eyes together, closed her mouth, and held her breath. The liquid burned her skin. When she thought they had stopped covering her in vile smelling chemicals, another porter poured even more of it over her. She barely had chance to take a deep breath and hold it again. Yet the acrid stink of the disinfectant burned her nose and eyes so much that it was hard to keep her mouth shut. Her uniform clung to her body and the wet fabric stung like acid.

Then they pointed the hose at her and jetted her with water again. Shocked, Evie took a deep breath filled with water. She coughed and spluttered so hard she thought she would suffocate.

When they were done, two porters hauled her to her feet and guided her to the washroom. Matron Davids followed, and when they were inside the small wash area, she said, "Strip off. Dump your uniform on the floor and dry yourself with the towels given. Dress in one of the dry porter coveralls provided." Then she closed the door behind her and left Evie shivering and alone in the room.

Evie stripped off every scrap of clothing, her skin still itching and burning where the chemicals had touched her. The skin under her arms was sore and red, but she didn't know if that was because of the disinfectant or the cold. Every inch of her hurt.

In the corner, a small showering unit stood over a small bathtub. She turned the water to hot and stepped under the spray. At first, only cold water came from the showerhead, but she didn't care. After a couple of minutes, the water warmed up a little and when it grew hot enough, she put the stopper in the bath. As she stood in the hot spray, the tub filled with warmth.

She used the soap provided and winced as she touched

the grazed skin on her knees and elbows. She dropped the soap into the holder and sank down into the bath.

There she curled up and hugged her knees to her chest. She stared at the tiled walls as the water surrounded her in soapy warmth and drops from the shower fell like warm rain upon her shoulders.

What's the point? she wondered. No matter what she did, it all seemed to go wrong. She closed her eyes to block out the world and let her thoughts drift in the warm comfort of the water.

7

Hesta sat in Jacobs' Tea House perusing the morning papers as she enjoyed a cup of Tanike Pink Tea. It was an expensive drink, but when made so that it filled her nose with the spices of the deserts she had only ever read about, it was worth every penny.

She scanned the front page, but nothing grabbed her attention. She checked the next few pages, then, noting the futility of finding anything to hold her attention, folded the paper for later. From her oversized bag, she removed two wax-sealed envelopes. One of them had been opened, the wax seal broken when she'd been with the family legal advisor, Mr Willard, and his junior associate Mr Abel Grimshaw. In fact, Mr Grimshaw had read it out and explained the legalities of the papers to her.

Even so, there seemed too much to grasp all at once. For one, she had the deeds in title for all of her brother's properties. She had access to all his funds, less the appropriate taxes, and so on. Godwyn had already arranged the services of an accountant with a firm in the city, and these financial services would validate all of Godwyn's holdings.

Her holdings now. She'd been well off before; now she need not work ever again.

Curiously, her brother had also left her another sealed envelope, which her legal representative refused to open. Godwyn had marked it 'private and confidential, for Hesta Bethwood's eyes only.' It sounded very clandestine.

Whereas the legal package had been thick and substantial, this particular envelope seemed strangely empty in comparison. Not only was it thin, it bore no marks as to what it might contain, other than her name. She stared at it for some minutes before she broken open the seal with a butter knife. Inside were letters to her—letters from Godwyn that he'd never sent. Maybe never intended to.

One letter contained instructions for the house at Queens Park and the ominous message that there would be more information in the safe there. He'd provided instructions, and she already had the safe key at home. Another letter outlined the properties he owned, the people staying in each one, and how much rent they needed to pay. There were more properties than she'd ever thought.

Her thoughts turned to Godwyn. He'd been so prepared for death. It was as if he'd known his days were numbered. She unfolded a handwritten note with the hope that a personal letter might give her more information. As she read this letter, it was as though she could hear him speaking the words.

"Dear sister, if you are reading this, then I am no longer with you. But I knew my time would be short. Given a chance, I would have given you a better warning, but these farseeing witches always want to withhold the details. I have made preparations as best I might given that I thought it was all hogwash. Be that as it may, there are important records in the safe of my house. This includes bills of sale and so on.

Also the people I employ, their work, and the costs. It might be best to destroy these things after I am gone.

Take care, sister mine, forgive me for what I have done. You will understand it all soon. Godwyn."

H er first thought was not for Godwyn but for Evie, and her heart broke anew for the life that Evie had never had and the one into which she'd been forced.

As she thought of Evie, her mind filled with a scream of pain so powerful she had to hold her head. *"Hesta!"* she heard, like a cry for help. The sound carried such anguish she could barely sit upright

Arthur, the tea house proprietor, glided to her side. "Miss Bethwood, are you all right?"

She started to shake her head, but the pain left her dizzy. "No. I need my driver. Now. Please, Arthur, get Charlie. He's in the calash outside."

Hesta had no idea how long it took for Charlie to reach her. Her brain thudded, and she shivered with a chill cold enough for the grave.

"Miss Bethwood, let me help you to the carriage," Charlie said. She hadn't even noticed him arrive. She took his arm, and they shuffled outside.

"Home, Miss Bethwood, or do you need a medic?"

"Take me to Evie, Charlie. Get there as fast as you can."

"Ma'am? Miss Chester is training today at the hospital."

"Then get me there, and do it fast. I think she's in trouble."

Charlie jumped into the driver's seat, and before she knew it, they were racing through the streets. Her head started to clear, but still that feeling of cold and death persisted.

They came to a halt under the portico of the hospital, and Hesta jumped out of the carriage as fast as she could. "Wait for me," she told Charlie, then grabbed her skirts and raced inside.

There were lots of people inside the reception hall, but she recognised none of them. The signs didn't help much either. A porter noticed her and strode over. "Can I help you, ma'am?"

"I'm looking for a nurse, Evie Chester," she answered.

"Now, there are a great many nurses today," he said.

"She's a trainee. This is a matter of great urgency."

"One moment," he said, and retrieved a clipboard from the reception desk. "Yes, today is a mortuary visit."

"Where is that?"

"I'm sorry, ma'am, but the mortuary is not open to the public."

Hesta stared at him, and she could feel her gift rise. "Where. Is. She." Her voice sang to him, and his eyes glazed over. When his gaze cleared, he smiled, "This way, ma'am. I'll show you how to get there."

The cold of the basement filled Hesta with a chill that seeped into her bones and filled her with dread.

"It's all right, I can find my way from here," she said.

The porter turned around and left her where she stood without saying a word.

Hesta took a deep breath; what would she say to anyone she saw? She'd think of something, she knew, and pushed her way through the mortuary doors as though she'd done the same thing a dozen times before.

Several things called for her attention as she stepped through the doors. The chill of the huge room made her shiver; she saw the doors of the dead on the walls, and the slippery floor, sodden with water, was not as she expected. The smell of disinfectant filled the air, and her breath came in puffs of steam.

There were people at the other end of the room, and they seemed intent on mopping the floor with such lackluster attention, they would take all day to get nowhere.

She would have liked to have crossed the room with confidence and a determined stride, but the slippery floor did not permit any kind of carelessness, so she kept her pace slow and deliberate.

"You," she said when she came to the nearest of the men—a porter, she decided by his dress. "I'm looking for a nurse. She was down here."

"They're all upstairs 'cept the one in the washroom," he said, and pointed.

"Thank you."

"But you can't go in there," he added.

Hesta didn't listen; she knew that the 'one in the washroom,' as he put it, had to be Evie. She didn't know how she knew; she just did.

The washroom door was unlocked, so she went straight inside. It was a small room, containing a wash basin, several hooks for clothing, a rack of towels, and a few dry coveralls. She saw a wet uniform dumped on the floor next to a wash basket for discarded clothing. A retaining wall enclosed the shower still running at the end of the room.

"Evie?"

She waited for a response, but no one replied. Hesta took a deep breath and strode over to the shower. There she found Evie, curled up in the bathtub, with tepid water running from the tap. The tub was almost overflowing.

"Evie!" she said. She grabbed a towel in one hand and turned off the water with the other. Evie looked up at her with bloodshot eyes. They almost matched the redness of her skin and the grazes that ran across her shoulders. "What happened?"

Evie sniffled and hugged her knees even tighter. She trembled so badly the water rippled with every little shake.

Hesta knelt down and ignored the water that seeped through her skirts. "It's all right, I'm here now. I'll take care of you."

She draped the towel around Evie's shoulders and started to lift her out of the water. "Come on, Evie, help me get you out of here and into some warm dry clothes. The water's getting cold."

Evie stood up, but she wouldn't look any higher than the floor.

"What did they do to you?" Hesta asked. She didn't expect a reply, but Evie shook her head.

"Come on, out of the water," Hesta urged, her voice low.

It took Evie a moment or two, and then she stepped out. Hesta grabbed another of the rather rough towels and used it to help Evie dry. Modesty meant little right then, and when Evie leaned against her, Hesta wrapped her arms around her and held her close. Evie shook so much it broke Hesta's heart, but there was nothing she could do except hold her and wait for the shivers to pass.

"I'm all right," Evie whispered. Then she stepped away. She pulled the towel around her, and with nervous eyes examined the room. Hesta stepped back; Evie was like someone cornered and terrified.

"Why are you here?" Evie asked.

"Because you called."

"I didn't." She stilled. "How did I call?"

Hesta tapped her head, and then the middle of her chest. "You called out in pain, and I came as fast as I could."

"You did?" Then Evie smiled, a shy, almost coy expression. "You did, too. For me?"

"I did."

That made her smile even more, but she also turned an indelicate shade of pink. "Thank you."

"You're hurt. Do you want to tell me what happened, or shall we get your injuries attended to?"

Evie shook her head. "I need to get my clothes."

"Where are they? I see only overalls here."

"They're upstairs in the staff room," Evie said.

"So do you want to dress in the porter's clothing and we'll

47

both go upstairs? Or do you want to wait here and I'll fetch them?"

"Don't leave me!" Evie almost cried.

"Then let's get you dried and dressed, even if it's in these things."

Evie dropped the towels on the floor and stood there naked. Heat rose into Hesta's cheeks, and she turned around before she stared. "I'll get you the porter clothes," she said. Even when she had the dry things in her hands, she walked backwards so she did not peek and held the clothing behind her.

"I'm decent now, you can turn around," Evie said. "I didn't know I was so scary."

"You aren't. Well, you are," Hesta started, but she grew more flustered by the moment.

"Have you never seen anyone naked?"

"Yes. No, I…" Hesta said, and the heat in her cheeks grew even hotter.

"Hesta Bethwood, I never pegged you for being shy," Evie said. "I've been a slave too long to worry about the state of my dress. I shall be more circumspect next time."

"No, you don't understand."

"Perhaps not."

"You have a lot of sores and redness. You look hurt. It needs to be attended to," Hesta managed to say.

"It's no good asking you, then, is it? You'd be terrified to see any uncovered skin."

Hesta took a deep breath. "Evie Chester, I can quite manage a little first aid. We'll take a look when we get home, shall we?"

"Clothes first," Evie said. "You will come with me?"

Hesta nodded. "Of course. And maybe you'll tell me who did this to you as well. I'd like to give them a piece of my mind."

Evie grabbed her arm and held on. "No, please, don't say anything. It's not worth it."

Hesta faced Evie and took a step closer. "Look at me."

At first, Evie didn't respond.

"Please," Hesta said softly.

When Evie looked up, Hesta smiled. "Of course, it's worth it. They hurt you, and they must be held accountable. At the very least, they should apologize for hurting you and leaving you alone without help."

"Thank you," Evie said.

Hesta stroked the side of Evie's face with the back of her hand. "There's no need. Just call me, and I'll come."

Evie threw her arms around Hesta and held on to her.

At first, Hesta wasn't sure what to do, and then she hugged her back. Evie needed her.

8

E vie let go of Hesta with some reluctance. She'd hugged Hesta only once before, and before that she'd only ever hugged Florie. Even then, touching Florie had worried her in case it triggered her gift and she purged into her without thinking. She could also infect at will, and the thought of all she had done, even though she'd been a slave and forced to do it by Godwyn, filled her with regret. With Hesta, so far she'd been able to enjoy the contact, and nothing untoward had happened. So far. But there remained the fear that something might.

It was nice to not feel quite so alone, but it reminded her how empty her life was. Would she have to return to that emptiness, or would this cozy feeling remain? Or would she forget herself one day and infect Hesta, too? A wave of cold raced through her, but she didn't want to think about it, not now she'd had a hint of what life could be like with people around her.

She straightened the overalls that covered her to the knees like a baggy and misshapen dress. It was as flattering as a sack, but a little less scratchy. Her shoes were soaked through, and she had no great urge to wear them. It would be unpleasant. All that remained were a pair of porter's rubberized boots. Like the overalls, they were too large for her, but she clumped about the washroom and didn't fall over. They would suffice.

"Are you ready to leave?" Hesta asked.

"How do I look?"

"Stunning," Hesta said.

"Good. Let's show the good people of the hospital a fine pair of lady's legs."

"Perfect. Let's go." Hesta grabbed Evie's wet shoes and held them away from her side, where they dripped with metronomic regularity.

Evie took Hesta's hand and led the way out of the washroom. She paused halfway across the mortuary. "I want to show you something."

The broom was not where she'd left it, and the doors to the autopsy room had been wedged open. "He's gone," Evie said. A ripple of fear rode along her spine and goosebumps erupted along her arms. Bodies didn't just go away.

"Who's gone?"

"The body from last night. He'd been attacked by the killer in the paper." She wandered into the room, but it had been washed down, and the stench of disinfectant made her eyes water. "They took him away."

Hesta looked around the mortuary. "Maybe he's in one of the drawers?"

"Maybe. Can you read the labels?"

"Yes, what are you looking for? Did you catch the name?"

Evie shook her head.

A porter—George—pushed the double doors open and strolled in. "Miss Chester, are you all right?"

"No, George, they very nearly killed me."

He looked away. "I'm sorry. The procedures for contaminated bodies are very clear. I'm sorry it hurt you. I've been caught once before and the disinfectant near took my eyes out."

"What happened to the body?" Evie asked.

"They burned it," he answered.

"Just like that?" Hesta asked.

"Yes, miss. Part of procedures when something is considered seriously wrong."

Hesta looked at Evie. "Let's get you dressed properly, and we'll ask the dean."

"Oh, you can't ask him," George said.

"Why not?" Evie asked.

"Well, he's the dean, isn't he? He'll be too busy for such things."

"Of course," Evie said. She smiled. "I wouldn't dream of bothering such a busy man."

He looked relieved at that.

"Good luck, George. See you another time, maybe."

"Right you are, Nurse Chester."

"At this rate, I'll never survive long enough to be a nurse." She grabbed Hesta's hand and marched towards the doors. "I need to get proper clothes. I don't mind the lack of shoes, but this scratchy thing is horrid."

Hesta held the sodden shoes. "I'm not sure if these will survive, either."

"They better. They're the only pair I have."

"We'll get you new ones."

"I can't afford—"

"Yes, you can. But we'll talk about that after we leave."

After many strange looks from patients, medics, and porters alike, they reached the staff room. Inside, Matron Davids sat upon one of few seats in the room, her elbow on the nearby table and a manila file on her lap.

She looked up as Evie and Hesta approached. "So you're washed, then."

"I think you were trying to kill me," Evie said.

"Seriously, what in hell is going on?" Hesta asked.

Davids closed the folder and placed it on the desk with several others. "Doctor Montgomery suggested that I might be frank with you, Evie."

"That would include Hesta Bethwood," Evie said.

"Very well." Davids gestured to the two remaining seats in the room. "It's awkward, really, but the official line must be that the poor fellow had been in contact with some plague, obviously from some foreign ship, and we'll have to run tests on people to make sure the disease has not spread."

"That's a lie," Evie said.

"Yes, of course it's a lie," Davids said. "But what else do we tell them?"

"The truth?" Hesta asked.

Davids turned her attention to Hesta. "And what truth would that be, Miss Bethwood? That the Butcher of Bristelle affects bodies in such a way that they do not conform to the normal stages of death? Is this merely a medical curiosity, or something more sinister? Or…" Her voice trailed off.

"Or what?" Hesta pressed.

"Or should we tell them that we fear this body, dead though it might be, has within it a life that is unnatural and might not remain in such a state long enough to be buried?"

"He wasn't dead, was he?" Evie asked.

Davids looked uncomfortable. "Yes. No. Who's to say?"

"At the very least you should tell people that there is some strangeness associated with the poor fellow," Hesta said.

"We always act in the interests of the common good," Davids said.

"So you burned him," Evie stated.

"For safety. And everything and everyone has been disinfected. You, of course, must go home and contact us if your health changes."

Evie snorted. "In case I have the contagion and die?"

Davids shook her head. "In case you die and get up and

53

walk again. Such behaviour is most difficult to explain in a hospital, so we'd rather not see it happen."

"It seems to me there is a great deal going on in this hospital that the general populace would find most odd," Hesta said.

"And you would be right," Davids said. "We have these processes and procedures in place for a very good reason. It's not whimsy."

"Maybe you should speak to experts about such issues," Hesta said.

"And who would such experts be?" Davids asked.

"The gifted?" Hesta suggested. "There are the towers and a few places in Knaresville where they can be found."

Now it was Davids who snorted her opinion on the matter. "Gifted? So speaks the sister of the man who would make them the finest citizens in all of Bristelle. I think you should find out who makes these strange things happen. I promise you it will be one of the so-called gifted who is to blame."

"I'm not sure I'd agree with you, matron," Evie said, "but if there are strange happenings, then an expert is needed."

"Find one," Davids answered. "But until then, burning solves all matters of uncertainty."

"Perhaps you're right," Hesta said.

"I am."

"And, of course, you're busy." She turned to Evie. "Better get dressed. I'll take you to my house where we can watch for any signs of infection."

Davids nodded. "So wise. Now, you should leave. I'll send you a list of books and suitable instructions for when you are deemed safe enough to return to the wards. We'll get you to observe a dissection some other time."

9

At Bethwood House, Evie slumped onto the couch in the drawing room and tucked her bare feet underneath her. Right then, all she wanted was for the earth to swallow her up. She hurt. Inside and out. Pain filled her. Cold, too. A chill seeped into her bones and she shivered.

She barely noticed when Hesta left the room, only realising it when she returned with Charlie in tow.

"Tea will be ready in a few minutes," she said.

Evie nodded.

"Miss Chester," Charlie said in greeting. He turned his attention to the unlit stove. It didn't take long before there was a fire roaring. "Plenty of wood here, Miss Bethwood. I'll bring a scuttle of coal and keep you stocked."

"Thank you, Charlie," Hesta said. "Go get yourself a cup of tea."

"Yes, Miss Bethwood," he said, and left.

"How are you feeling?" Hesta asked.

Evie wanted to keep her despair to herself. It filled her with such hopelessness. Every time she took a step forward, someone or something not only pushed her back, but did so with force. It was always painful and violent. She couldn't win. And she couldn't talk about it.

"Evie…" Hesta prompted.

"I feel like hell," she admitted. "No matter what I do, it only ever gets worse."

"No, it doesn't. Not always. There are always ups and downs."

"I think I should be the judge of my life. Trust me, it is always bad. I've had enough of it."

"No, you haven't."

Evie stiffened and turned to face her. A part of her wanted to shout, What did she know anyway? Then she saw the concern in Hesta's eyes. For once, someone seemed to care about her, and Evie almost lost it. Warmth filled her and caught, like an ache, at the back of her throat. Her eyes stung and her vision wavered.

Hesta looked away, as though she knew Evie couldn't hold back her tears.

Evie had to take a moment to make sure she could speak without giving away her emotional state. "Well, that's my nursing career stuffed up already," she said.

"No, it isn't. It just means it will take a little longer."

"Dammit, Hesta!"

"You could start reading the books. I have a few in the library that might help. One is on anatomy."

"Hesta," Evie closed her eyes and pinched the bridge of her nose, "I'm never going to get anywhere here. I can't read, and I would be gifted in a place where they don't want it. It's going to kill me to be surrounded by people dying from something I could so readily fix."

Hesta moved to her side and patted Evie's knee. "And the problem is?"

Evie glared at her. Anger was so much better than feeling sorry for herself.

"Well, we'll talk about that later, shall we? Meanwhile,

let me show you." From the sideboard next to the door, Hesta grabbed a collection of books. When she sat back on the couch, she put the books in a pile at her feet and reached for the topmost tome. "I set aside a few books that I thought might be interesting. Like this one. It's about anatomy." She opened the book to a random page, and a detailed sketch showed the musculature of the chest in detail.

"Look, from this we can see the serratus anterior, external and internal intercostals, and all the rest," Hesta said.

Evie grunted her response.

"Well, maybe later."

"Maybe," Evie agreed.

"How are your sores? I can get some ointment to make them feel better. They looked raw earlier, and I wouldn't want them to get infected."

"I don't get infections," she said. Except when she didn't purge, and then all kinds of things happened. Most of them unpleasant.

"Except when you don't purge," Hesta said, as though she read Evie's mind.

"Except for then."

"We'll just have to make sure you purge properly, then. Your bruises will still need attention. At the very least, it would help you with the pain."

"The pain is all over. It will heal. It always does."

"Let me help." Hesta reached out and touched her hand. "Please?"

Evie had to think about it for a moment. The ache in her throat had started again, and she had to be sure she could speak without tears. "All right, then, if it will help."

"It will." Hesta squeezed her hand once more. "You could do with wearing loose clothing, too."

"I don't have—"

"I know, but how about a night shirt? It would give you

some cover as I put on the salve." She stood up. "Let me get it while we're waiting for the tea. I won't be but a moment."

As Hesta left the room, a matronly woman with dark hair tied in a bun brought in a tray with tea. She pulled out an occasional table and set it before the couch.

"Thank you," Evie said.

Mrs Dunn smiled. "Shall I pour you a cup?"

"Thank you, no. I'll wait for Hesta," Evie answered.

"As you wish." She backed towards the door and closed it on the way out.

Evie stared at the tea tray, and when the tea didn't pour itself, she sat upright at the edge of her seat and checked the contents of the tray. The tea cosy fit the teapot exactly, as though made specifically for this one pot, which was taller and slimmer than all the teapots she'd ever seen.

Evie stared straight ahead, her eyes unfocussed and her hand loosely resting where Hesta had sat. She had to wonder why Hesta took so long, the room was empty without her there.

Just as Evie's mood began to sink a little more, Hesta breezed into the room and brought with her hope and sunshine. She had a loose shirt over one arm and carried a small white box under the other.

"Ahh, tea is ready. Good. Shall I pour whilst you get changed into this?" Hesta handed her the nightgown. "It might be a little large for you, but it will do for now."

Evie stared at the gown but didn't move.

"I've told Mrs Dunn not to disturb us," Hesta added. "No one will come in at an inopportune moment and see you in a state of undress."

"It's not necessar—"

"I think it is," Hesta interrupted. "Do you want me to leave whilst you get changed?"

"No. Yes. I don't know," Evie replied.

Hesta sat on the edge of the couch. "I'll pour the tea, shall I?"

"Yes."

Hesta readied the cups, checked that the tea had been infused, and poured two cups. "Do you need help to get changed?"

"Yes, all right."

Evie didn't move, but Hesta stood up and offered her hand. "Stand."

Getting undressed was more about Hesta undressing her, as though Evie had become a lady with an attendant to take care of her. She closed her eyes and let the dream wipe away the darkness, even if only for a moment or two. It was a nice dream. She began to unfasten her own buttons, but her hands trembled so much that Hesta stopped her.

"It's all right. You're hurt and that always take it out of you." She loosened all of the buttons and fastenings on Evie's clothing and turned around. "Slip out of that, and get the nightgown on. I'll throw a couple of logs onto the fire."

Evie rushed to shed her clothing and don the nightshirt. It was roomy and loose, like all such clothes, but was obviously made for someone with more curves than her diminutive frame possessed.

"Ready," she said. She piled her clothing to one side and sipped at her tea. Hesta had sweetened it, and it was lovely.

"Let's see. Well, that doesn't fit too badly, now does it?"

"No, it's good, thank you."

"It's one of my spares, and I thought it might be too big for you."

"Yours?" Evie asked. Warmth crept through her entire body. This nightwear had been worn by Hesta.

Hesta opened the wooden box and selected a jar of salve from inside. "Now, where shall I start? Where does it hurt the most?"

Heat rose into Evie's cheeks. "My back, I think."

Hesta stared at her for a moment. "Well, the shirt doesn't help when it comes to getting to your back. I didn't think it through, really."

Evie adjusted herself so that the gown bunched up behind her. She leaned forward and lifted the cotton so she uncovered a small area at the base of her back. "There."

Hesta's warm hands raised the shirt and exposed more of Evie's skin. Even though the fire added warmth to the room, the air felt cool to her damaged flesh.

"Dear Mother," Hesta said. "Did they beat you as well?"

"No. The water jet was powerful though. It knocked me around a lot."

"Right, I didn't see this much when I found you in the washroom."

"It's probably just showing up now," Evie said, and rested her forehead against the back of the couch.

She hissed when Hesta touched her back, but when the salve eased her sores she closed her eyes, and her muscles relaxed.

"Does it still hurt?" Hesta asked.

"Not anymore," she said.

Hesta moved the shirt higher and held it whilst she rubbed a little salve into a cut. "Dammit," she said as she dropped the jar. "I need another pair of hands."

As she picked up the jar, Evie gathered the nightshirt in both hands and pulled it over her head.

"Evie, what are you doing?"

"Making it easier for you."

"Oh."

Evie turned around and sat on the edge of the seat. She gathered the nightshirt together and held it in front of her, her back and shoulders fully exposed. "Is that too improper?"

Hesta shook her head rapidly, but her cheeks had reddened and she refused to look Evie in the eye. She picked up the jar of ointment and for a moment stared at the contents.

"Is something wrong?" Evie asked.

Hesta sighed. "I think you should turn around so I can finish your back."

She put a good dollop of salve on Evie's shoulder and massaged the ointment into the side of her neck, over her shoulder, and part way down her arm. To Evie, it seemed that Hesta took her time at her neck. The sensation was nice and soothing. Then she applied more over her back and stopped only a little way above Evie's underthings.

"It's done."

Evie didn't move for a moment as she relished the comfort of the cream and Hesta's attentions. It was nice; more than nice, in fact. She turned around, the shirt still in her hands, and sat on the edge of the couch. Even now, Hesta would not look her in the eye.

"Do I bother you?"

"No, not at all."

"But you won't look at me."

"You don't understand," Hesta said. "You are…" She waved her free hand around in lieu of words.

"I'm what?"

Hesta shook her head. "Do you feel any relief from your hurts?"

Evie cocked her head to one side and lowered the nightdress. She watched Hesta's reactions as she pointed to her collar bone. "How about this here?"

"I can't see any—"

"But it hurts."

Hesta gulped, but she added salve to both sides and hastily rubbed the ointment into Evie's skin. "Better?"

Evie pointed to her knees. "Here."

"I thought you could do that yourself. You can reach those."

"But you do it so much better than I would," she said softly. "And I like it when you do it."

Hesta stared at Evie's knees. "What are you doing, Evie? Are you teasing me?"

Evie thought it over for a moment. "Maybe. I'm not sure what I'm doing."

Hesta stood up and took a few steps backwards, moving so quickly she almost knocked the tea over. Evie's stomach dropped. Had she misunderstood all of Hesta's words and actions?

Heat rose into her cheeks in a burning wave. Evie had thought she meant more to Hesta, because no one cared for her as much as Hesta did.

"I'm sorry, I didn't mean to offend." She stood up and turned away long enough to get the nightshirt back over her head. "Let me get my clothes on and I'll be off."

"No," Hesta said. "You don't understand."

"Yes, I do. I've been privy to quite a lot as I've travelled from house to house and been sold to a room full of gents who got caught with something nasty."

Hesta winced at the implicit accusation. "That's not what I mean either."

"Then explain it to me."

"I worry you'll think I'm taking advantage of you. Because I'm not sure if you trust me yet."

"Oh." Evie picked up her cup of tea and took a sip of the cooling drink. She hadn't expected Hesta to say anything like that.

"There you have it. Here you are, half undressed, and I shall act like the perfect gentleman and not take advantage of your state."

"Well, I don't want you to be a gentleman, because then you wouldn't be you."

"Thank you."

Evie thought she looked relieved to hear that. "But I can see the sense in what you say."

"Thank you for that, as well," Hesta said.

"In that case, can I take you out to dinner sometime?"

Hesta looked into Evie's eyes and answered without hesitation. "Yes."

Evie moved closer. "Remember what I said about the next time?"

"Next time?"

Evie hooked her hand around the back of Hesta's neck to pull her head down a little. She lifted up on her tiptoes and brushed her lips against Hesta's. "I said the next time, it would be me that kissed you."

Hesta's smile filled the room with brightness. "Indeed you did. Is it my turn next?"

"We'll see," Evie replied. "But don't go expecting kisses all of the time."

10

Not for the first time, Hesta woke up with Evie asleep against her shoulder. She liked it, and the smile that broke out over her face grew so broad it almost hurt. She needed someone in her life, someone she could trust and share things with, especially now that her brother was no longer with them. Her smile faded at the thought of Godwyn and how he'd died.

She turned her attention to Evie; her light hair and light skin looked so delicate. It was almost impossible to think she had lived the life she'd had, and survived.

Evie's eyelids fluttered open, and a pair of bright blue eyes stared into her own.

"Hesta, what's wrong?" Evie asked. Then she yawned.

"Nothing," she replied. "I didn't realise you were already awake."

Evie yawned again and sat up. "We fell asleep on the couch again."

"What you really mean is that you fell asleep and I didn't have the heart to move you."

"Suits me." Evie stretched. "I've slept in worst places."

"I suppose I should be grateful you no longer view me and my shoulder as the worst place."

"There is that."

Hesta straightened her skirts. "And at least you slept in a nightshirt. That's a far more comfortable option."

"I'm sorry. Did you sleep at all?" Evie asked.

"A little," she answered. Hesta didn't add that she was stiff and sore from sitting upright. Evie had needed her, and she wasn't going to let her down no matter how much discomfort she might endure.

"It's early still, and you had a rough day yesterday. Do you want to go upstairs and sleep a little longer?"

"I'm fine. If this were a normal and ordinary day, then I'd be ready for whatever I had to do. These days that would mean being ready for my shift at the hospital. Now I'm awake, so I might as well stay awake."

"All right, if that's what you want."

"What about you?" Evie asked.

"I didn't get beaten by water jets." Hesta smiled. "Can I check your injuries?"

Evie rose to her feet and pulled her nightshirt up and over her back.

Hesta looked away at first; the sight of Evie's back brought that familiar searing heat into her cheeks. She coughed into her hand and stood up. She tried not to pay any attention to the outline of her ribs, nor the shape of her spine pressing against her skin. Evie needed feeding up, that was for sure. Thankfully, the injuries looked to be healing well. "You were right about healing fast. And no sign of redness or infection."

"Told you," Evie said.

Hesta reached out and brushed her fingers over Evie's shoulder blade. "I thought this part here would take longer to close. It was raw."

Evie shrugged.

"Does it hurt?"

"No. The salve helped."

"Possibly," Hesta agreed. "Could your gift tell you if you were infected?"

"Usually I know when I'm exposed to something. But I don't know if that means I would recognise all infections or diseases. Sometimes I need to know what the problem is before I notice there's an issue."

"Either way, I'm glad you're recovering, and I hope that's as bad as it gets."

"Me too. I'm hungry, though."

"Let's go and see what we can find in the kitchen, shall we?"

Evie followed Hesta through the house. "I never refuse food or a trip to a kitchen," Evie said.

Hesta had barely had a chance to slice a round of bread when Mrs Dunn bustled into the kitchen. "Miss Bethwood, what do you think you're doing?"

"Breakfast," Hesta said.

"If I'd have known you intended to rise so early, I would have prepared for that." Mrs Dunn shook her head. "Sit. I'll make tea, and I'll toast that bread for you, Miss Chester."

"You mean you don't want me to make a mess?" Hesta asked.

"It's better if I keep on top of things myself, Miss Bethwood. If everyone just helps themselves to everything, then we'll end up in a right pickle, won't we?"

"Of course," Hesta agreed.

Mrs Dunn turned away and busied herself with the stove. She opened the vents and added wood. "Won't be a moment. Charlie banked the fire earlier so that it would be nice and hot when I started for the day."

"That's fine. Mrs Dunn, do we have anything Evie might be able to wear? After yesterday, I'm not sure she can use her own things."

Mrs Dunn looked Evie up and down. "Quite right. Small. I don't really have anything." She looked thoughtful for a moment. "Although I do have a pair of trousers that needed mending for my nephew. I know it's boys' clothes but they are much the same size. It'll get you by until you can get proper clothes."

"Is that all right with you, Evie?" Hesta asked.

"Yes. I need to buy clothes soon," Evie said, "I just seem to forget."

"Mrs Dunn, do you know a seamstress who has time to make clothes for Evie—sooner rather than later?" Hesta asked.

Mrs Dunn nodded. "I can fix what needs mending, but I know someone who can make things from scratch, like."

"Good." She turned her attention to Evie, "There is a shop in one of the side streets of Salverton. I often go there, but they have a waiting list. They also prefer to make a particular type of clothing, and I am not sure you would be interested just yet."

"You mean they are expensive, and I'm not an expensive clothing kind of woman?"

"No, I mean they make mostly evening dresses and formalwear. Sometimes a decent dress can be found off the peg."

"Oh, I see," Evie said.

"Would you prefer to get something off the peg from one of the stores?"

"I've never bought my own clothes before," Evie said.

"In that case, what if I got Mrs Dunn to alter one of my dresses to fit you, and then we can get more from a shop until you feel you want a seamstress to make them for you?"

Evie nodded.

"Right then, Mrs Dunn, if you could make an introduction to your seamstress, I would be much obliged," Hesta said.

"And rather than bother you any more, we'll be in the parlour when the tea is ready."

"As you like," she replied.

Evie grabbed the slice of bread and took a huge bite.

"I was going to toast that for you!" Mrs Dunn said.

"Hungry," Evie said through a mouthful.

"She'll have more, Mrs Dunn," Hesta said. "Evie is hollow."

In the parlour, Hesta sat next to the fireplace and watched Evie cram food into her mouth as quickly as she could. "You'll make yourself sick."

Evie shook her head.

"Are you all right?" Hesta asked.

Evie nodded.

"Will you stay here today?"

Evie shrugged. "Could do. I've nothing better to do."

"Such a glowing endorsement."

"What?"

Hesta ignored the look on Evie's face. "No matter. You are supposed to stay indoors to make sure you don't show signs of some weird infection."

"I don't get infections," Evie said.

"I know, but we'd better be certain, eh?"

"All right, then."

"It doesn't mean we have to sit here and stare at the walls until we go crazy. There are things we can do," Hesta said.

"Such as?"

"For a start, we could find out about this body that didn't act like a proper dead body."

"Yes, but how? I can't look at him now."

"True, but we can look into the principle of the thing. We can go through the library. I can read while you practice your reading and writing, and then I'll show you some books that might help." She held up a hand. "And before you say anything about not being able to read, I'll help you."

"All right," Evie said. "But you might want to get a hold of your brother's men and get them to find out the news on the streets."

"You know, Evie, I think that's a great idea. I need to take control of all his assets."

"Now you sound like him."

Hesta snorted. "He employs…employed people. They'll all need to know where they stand, and if they have employment or a roof over their heads going forward."

Evie froze in her seat. "I'm sorry."

Hesta patted Evie's knee. "Let me get a few things set up, and then we can focus on you and seeing what we can find out."

Evie stared at the floor. "All right."

"And I promise, if there is no sign of anything strange, then tomorrow we'll do something different."

Evie nodded with enthusiasm. "Yes, that would be good."

"Right, stay there, be comfortable, and I'll be right back." Hesta left Evie curled up on the couch. She went to see Mrs Dunn in the kitchen first, and Charlie came in for his morning tea just as she arrived. "Charlie, we're staying indoors today on account of Miss Chester's health. I need you to run some messages and errands for me, if you will."

"Of course, miss. Just tell me what you need doing, and I'll make it done."

She smiled. "Thank you, Charlie. First, I need you to go to Evie's house and tell Mrs Hickman that Evie is fine but she has an infection. She'll stay with me until she's better. Also, fetch any clothing that Evie has there."

"Right, I'll do that."

"I also want to see whoever Godwyn's right-hand man was." She had to think for a moment to see if she could recall the details from the paperwork she'd acquired.

"I suggest Mr Grobber," Charlie said.

"Then summon Mr Grobber here so I can assert my control as head of the business."

"Of course, Miss Bethwood."

Hesta looked up from her book. Evie sat in her own chair; she still wore her borrowed trousers and sat with her legs tucked underneath her. She stared at the anatomy book she had open in front of her and recited the names she had memorised of the human skeleton. After only two days, Evie probably knew the name of every bone in the body already, not to mention a selection of blood vessels and muscles. Her curiosity and desire to learn things had surpassed insatiable and was moving rapidly towards obsessed.

"Hesta, what's this word?" Evie asked, and not for the first time.

When Hesta looked over Evie's shoulder, she saw a rather detailed drawing of a heart.

"What's that say?" Evie pressed.

Hesta sighed. "I know you want to learn, but it would be better to practice your reading with words that aren't from a specialist language. If you get more normal words mastered, then this will be so much easier."

"But I want to know how it all works," Evie said.

"Yes, I know, but let's try something ordinary to start. You don't need to know everything all at once".

Evie frowned at her, but Hesta wouldn't let her grumpiness interfere with the point she was making. She pulled out one of the journals, one written by a younger girl as she found her gift. Of all the books Hesta owned, this one didn't use any special language, and she hoped Evie would be able to work her way through the diary on her own well enough to increase her confidence and her skill.

"All right, if you think it will help," Evie conceded, and concentrated on the words on the pages of the new book.

"When you come across a word you don't know, write it down and we can make it a learning word."

Hesta looked up at the sound of the doorbell being rung—they didn't have many visitors, generally—but turned her attention back to her book. A few minutes later, she heard voices and Mrs Dunn opened the door to the library.

"Miss Bethwood. A Mr Grobber is here."

Evie jerked upright. "Grobber is here?"

"Show him in, thank you," Hesta said.

Mr Grobber was exactly as Hesta remembered, and from the look of horror on Evie's face, she remembered him, too. He wore a suit and carried a small cap in hand. At least he knew his manners.

He bobbed his head as he entered the room. "Miss Bethwood." Then he bobbed his head towards Evie. "Miss Chester."

Hesta regarded him thoughtfully. "Mr Grobber, my brother is dead."

"Yes, ma'am. My condolences."

"Thank you," Hesta said. She took a moment to compose herself. "You may not yet be aware, but I am the beneficiary of his entire estate."

Grobber didn't respond to that. Not that there was much he could say or do about it.

"So, rather than upset everything, I need to know how he operated and who did what. He made some notes for me, but I have yet to tour his holdings. Undoubtedly, the king's accountants will claim taxes and so forth, and I must prepare and understand the nature of my holdings before I'm bled dry."

"Of course, Miss Bethwood. I understand that Mr Bethwood kept a full accounting of his business in his house safe."

"That is as I understand, but I have not yet visited his house."

He looked as though he wanted to tell her what to do and then changed his mind. "How can I help?" he asked instead.

"First, let it be known to all employees that employment will continue unless it is illegal or useless."

"Thank you, ma'am. I'll spread the word."

Hesta nodded. "Who collected the rents, and when?"

"Me and Mr Wiggins would collect on the first day of every month," he replied. "We would write everything down in a book as we collected the money."

"And Godwyn trusted you with that job?"

"Yes, ma'am, although sometimes he came with us in the coach."

"To make sure you collected the right money?"

He stared at the floor. "No, ma'am. To scare them if they were awkward, like."

"So, the first of the month. That gives us a couple of weeks before we collect again."

"Yes, ma'am."

"And who gathered the news on the street?" Hesta asked.

"We have a number of people we could ask when needed."

"Good," she said. She thought for a moment. "I have need of information. Can you find out anything, no matter how odd the request?"

"If there is something you need to know, I know someone who can find it for you," he said.

She nodded. "If I asked you to find out everything you could about these murders, the ones where the victim is being ripped apart as though by a beast, you could find out about that?"

He nodded. "That one would be easy. Everyone is talking about it."

"Oh, are they?"

"Many of the folk of Bristelle work nights, see, and it's not safe."

"Street walkers?" Evie prompted.

"Yes, Miss Chester. The ladies are loath to work without protection, especially at the moment."

"I would like to talk with these ladies," Hesta said. "To see what they know."

Grobber looked horrified. "I'm sure, miss, but these are not the kind of ladies you pass the time of day with in casual conversation."

"Of course not, Mr Grobber. Not when they only come out at night," Hesta said.

"But, Miss Bethwood, these parts of the business do not need your direct attention. I can quite readily run everything on your behalf."

As she thought about her response, words echoed inside her mind. '*Lying, scheming thug.*' Evie, it seemed, could communicate with her telepathically whenever she chose.

'*What do you think?*' she responded back.

'*He isn't offering to help for your benefit,*' Evie's thoughts came back.

"Thank you for your offer, Mr Grobber, but I intend to take a personal interest in all of my brother's affairs," she said.

"If that is what you wish," he replied, but he looked as though he'd tasted a mouthful of vinegar.

"Indeed I do," she said. "I have people on it already. Perhaps you had better make sure that all of our employees know exactly who the boss is. If they don't like it, they can leave, and if I find anything underhand, skimming the take, or so on, then I will take the matter through legal channels."

"I understand, Miss Bethwood," he said.

"I hope you do, and I hope the others do, too. Godwyn may have had a bigger physical presence, but my methods are more subtle and longer lasting. It would be best if everyone understood that."

"Yes, Miss Bethwood."

"Good. The next thing is that I want to speak with anyone who knows anything about the business and anything that might affect it."

Grobber nodded.

"I also wish to proceed with the academy for the gifted, so I need to speak with people who know about that, too."

"And where will you speak with them?" he asked.

"Here, of course," she replied.

"Perhaps they would like some place neutral," Evie suggested. "We could maybe set aside a time and go to that cafe down by the market at the east end of Ardmore."

"I know it. Everyone knows that place. It would be better than here," Grobber said. "It might be better to keep a pocket full of coppers, too. That will loosen tongues."

"Good. I would like to see the grapevine fully operational. It will help with this beast attack."

"Are you interested in that as well?"

"Yes. It affects business as much as anything else."

"I'll see what I can do," Grobber said.

"Good. Everything will come through me from now on, Mr Grobber. I will need a short while to get Godwyn's affairs in correct order, but I don't want anyone to suffer in the transition period. Speak with me if there are any issues."

"Of course, ma'am. I'll get on with it."

"Before you go, how many slaves are there?" Evie asked.

"Good question," Hesta said.

"There are no slaves in any of the Bethwood ventures," he replied. "Not since Evie and Florie."

Evie closed her eyes and smiled.

A knock at the door interrupted her thoughts, and Mrs Dunn poked her head into the room. "There's another gent here, a doctor, come to see you, Miss Bethwood."

"Mr Grobber is leaving now, I think, Mrs Dunn. If you could show him out and show the doctor in."

Grobber inclined his head in a shallow bow that seemed an inch shy of disrespectful.

"Find out what you can and come back in a day or two."

"Yes, ma'am."

She waited for the door to close behind him before she spoke to Evie. "Is that all right?"

"Yes. It's getting better, I think. But he's—"

"I know. I know," Hesta interrupted. "There is only so much for now. We'll cover that topic further when we are more settled."

The door swung open, and Mrs Dunn ushered in Doctor Montgomery. He bowed, a deep and respectful bow that included Evie as well as Hesta. Evie appreciated the gesture.

"Doctor, to what do we owe the pleasure of your visit?" Hesta asked.

"A number of things, really," he said. "First, how are you feeling, Miss Chester?"

"Very well, considering you tried to drown me."

He took a deep breath. "My apologies, but such is the protocol when faced with an infection of indeterminate origin and virility," he said. "We must protect all."

"I'm not prone to sickness," Evie said.

"So you say, but if you wish to be treated as any other nurse in training, then you must be treated in the same way no matter what."

"Makes sense," Hesta said.

"Apology accepted," Evie said. "When can I go back?"

"You are required to engage in a two-weeks quarantine, but I see that there are people coming and going regardless of our procedures."

Hesta shrugged. "If anyone gets infected with whatever it is, then we will deal with it."

"Doctor," Evie started, "you are far too busy to come all

this way to see how a nurse fares. What is the real purpose of your visit?"

"We have another body," he said, "and I need your help. I think the whole city needs your help. There is something most odd going on, and I worry for us all so much that I dare not take these bodies into the morgue for fear of what might happen in the rest of the hospital."

"What do you want me to do about it?" Evie asked.

"I am aware of what you can do, Miss Chester. Your demonstration in the infections ward was most instructive. I hope you can help us further. To do so, I've had the body moved to Rotunda Hall, where no one can see what is going on." He looked straight at Evie. "Please, Miss Chester, will you help?"

11

———————

E vie settled into the carriage as they headed through the
hospital and university grounds all the way towards
Rotunda Hall. Several porters stood outside the main
entrance, but the carriage didn't stop there. Instead, Joym
directed the driver to the rear entrance, where there was but a
single porter. A stout, grey-haired chap who peered at the
carriage as though he'd never seen one. Or perhaps as if he
couldn't see it too well.

"Esher, good man. Let us in, will you?" Joym said.

"Of course, Dean Montgomery." He looked at the two
women with the dean but thought better of asking why they
were with him. He stared at Evie for a moment, noticed her
trousers, and shook his head.

"There are a couple of things we need to do," Doctor
Montgomery said. "Lock the door after us, and don't let
anyone else in."

"It's cold inside, sir," Esher said. "There are no services
engaged at the moment."

"I am aware of that, and it is quite all right," Joym said.

Esher fumbled with a small bunch of keys attached to the
belt at his waist. He selected a thick key and inserted it into

the lock. He turned it, and with a distinct *clunk* the lock turned. He pulled the door open and let them in, then closed the door and locked it again behind them.

"Can we get out after?" Hesta asked.

"We most certainly can. I have my own keys, but it makes the porters feel important if they can unlock doors for us," Joym answered.

Inside, the darkened passageway led to the main theatre. A little light filtered in from the door, but not enough for them to see much. There were three doors before the amphitheater main floor: two to the right and one to the left.

Joym reached into his waistcoat pocket and pulled out a set of two keys. He inserted one key into the door on the left and disappeared into the dark interior. A loud *kerthunk* followed, and after a brief moment, the lights came on inside the hall.

"That's better," he said. "Are you ready for this?"

"Yes," Hesta said.

"Yes," Evie added. She pushed the shirt sleeves up her arms and rolled her shoulders. If this body was like the other one, she already knew what she sought. It would be quicker to see, she hoped.

Joym led the way, his leather shoes making little sound as he strode along the short passageway into the Rotunda. Dim, flickering light permeated the darkness of the entry and grew gradually brighter as the lights strengthened and the trio approached the inner section of the hall.

The room was as Evie remembered, although it seemed different now that they stood at the lowest level and she could stare at the tiers that stretched into the darkness. In the center of the demonstration area, a sheet-covered gurney shone in the reflection of the overhead lights. Under the sheet, the distinct shape of a body could be seen.

"Anything you need?" Joym asked, his voice quiet and his words almost whispered.

Evie shook her head as she focused her attention on the body.

Joym backed away and took a place on the lower audience tier. "Whenever you're ready," he said.

Hesta moved closer to Evie's side. "Are you all right?"

"I'm fine. What about you?"

"I've seen bodies before. Shall we get on with it?"

Evie stopped and looked at her. "Do you mean Godwyn and Ekvard."

"Yes."

"I'm sorry, truly I am."

Hesta reached out and touched Evie's arm. "I know you are. But it wasn't for nothing, was it? He died for something important."

"No, it wasn't for nothing."

Hesta let go of Evie's arm and made her way to the gurney. She looked over her shoulder at Evie and pulled the sheet from the body. The material slid to the ground as Hesta stared at what was revealed. Evie found herself rushing to place herself between Hesta and the deceased.

"I'm fine," Hesta said. In spite of her words, she looked away. "I didn't expect him to be naked."

Evie looked at the rather damaged body and laughed. "Hesta, seriously. Someone ripped him open, and you're more worried about his tadger being on show?"

"Well…"

Evie took one look at Hesta's face and led her away from the gurney, and just in time. As they reached the lower tier, Hesta retched and everything she'd eaten that morning splattered on the floor.

"It's all right," Evie soothed. "It's a lot to see all at once."

"I'll get some water," Joym said, and strode with haste from the hall.

Hesta leaned against the lower stands, her breath ragged

and deep. Evie didn't know what to do, so she rubbed her back.

"It's all right. We can leave," Evie said.

"No. I'm fine. I didn't expect this."

"What, the naked bit?"

"The blood, the smells, and him being so hurt," Hesta said. "Oh, Evie, he must have been in such pain and suffered so." She wrapped her arms around Evie and tucked her head against her neck.

Evie held Hesta lightly in her arms. The scent of Hesta and rosewater filled her nose. "You don't have to stay. I can deal with this."

Hesta stayed where she was, her breath growing steady against the side of Evie's neck. Then she pulled away and cool air touched Evie's skin where Hesta's breath had warmed her. Hesta didn't move her arms from around her, though, but held on as though she needed the contact.

"I'm fine. I will be fine," Hesta said, although it sounded as though she were trying to convince herself more than Evie. "And I must be with you at all times. I'll not be any use if I fail at the smallest sight of blood, now, will I?"

"It's not a small amount," Evie said.

"It's so red, and it looks so raw."

"It shouldn't be," Evie said.

Joym rushed back with a glass of water and a small hand towel.

"Thank you," Hesta said, as she accepted both the water and the towel. She rinsed her mouth and looked for a place to spit it out.

"On the floor is fine," Joym said.

She turned her back on Evie and the doctor and spit the whole lot onto the ground. She took several gulps of the water before she turned around. "I'm sorry to be so...weak."

"My dear, there is nothing to be sorry about," Joym said. "Not everyone has the stomach for such things."

"Just watch, it'll be all right. If you're here, I feel better anyway," Evie said.

"Do you?" The hope in Hesta's voice tore at Evie's heart.

"Of course." She smiled as best she could given that they were but a few feet from a dead body. "I better get on with this, though, and then we can leave."

She took a deep breath and turned her attention to the job at hand. "Who is, or was, he?"

"His name is Derek Monsin," Joym answered.

She walked around the gurney. "He's not very old, mid-twenties."

"Yes, I have his file on my desk, if you need it."

"No. It's not necessary. Has he had any kind of examination yet?" she asked.

"Only a cursory one. It seems pretty certain why he's dead."

"True enough." The lack of investigation suited Evie; there would be less chance for contamination if no one looked too closely. "He has dirt embedded in his hands. I can smell smoke, coal, and coke rather than wood. All stokers get this smell to them. It's like the smoke and the coal becomes a part of them."

"Correct. He was on his way home from the ironworks," Joym said.

"I'm impressed," Hesta said.

"Don't be. It's no more than simple observation," Evie said. Her attention remained on Derek. "There are three deep gashes running from the right and down." She shook her head as her clarified her thoughts. "Correction, it's *his* left. The gashes run across the upper part of the chest and the ribs. They look quite ragged, and they're deep enough to penetrate the sternum. I think they have exposed parts of the costal cartilage."

"Excellent," Joym said. "You have in your possession a greater knowledge of anatomy than I suspected."

"I've been studying."

"Good. Now, you can see why they feel it is some beast," Joym said.

"I agree. As to other factors, the pallor of the skin is not as pale as I would expect on someone of his complexion." She grabbed the sheet and used it to lift the man's arm. "No rigor, and I can see no signs of livor mortis either." She took a whiff of the body. "The smell, although not pleasant, is not as *un*pleasant as I would expect."

"I concur with all of your observations," Joym said.

Evie took a few steps backwards, and now, instead of holding back her gift, she let it stretch out. She'd seen this effect before. On the other body. The way it glittered with darkness to her gift-enhanced senses could not be mistaken. She reached out to touch his shoulder.

"No!" Hesta cried out.

Evie paused; her hand outstretched. "What?"

"You can't touch a dead person. You might...you might catch something."

"Actually, that's what I'm going to try to do," Evie replied and touched the body.

As before, the darkness within the body seemed to avoid her touch, and yet, in the back of her mind, it occurred to her that although the curse was hiding from her, it sought *someone*. Someone specific? Anyone other than her?

The realisation gave her some freedom. She need not fear touching the body, or any part of it. She stuck her finger inside one of the bloody gashes. The wound felt all too fresh, but Evie had seen and touched worse. As before, a flood of rage and pain roared through her mind, stronger than before. The pain of being rent apart almost threw her backwards, but she knew this force was was more about her own reaction. *Kill. Rip.*

"It's the same as the one before," she said.

"How is it like before?" Joym asked. "I missed your assessment."

Evie took several huge gulps of air before she spoke further. "None of this is natural. You can call it a beast as much as you like, because it is a kind of beast, but not one that is like any you or I might think of."

"What do you mean?" Joym asked.

"I don't know. All I feel is rage, the need to kill. This beast is a cursed one." She stopped to think for a moment. "Or it spreads through a curse."

"I'm not sure that helps much," he said. "One moment." He left to go into one of the side rooms.

Evie stared at the wounds. In the background, she could hear the clatter of medical instruments being hastily added to a dish. She waited for Joym to show her what he had in mind.

She'd been correct about the instruments. She had no idea what any of them were, but he donned a pair of white gloves and put the small tray on the side of the gurney.

"It's a pity we aren't in an autopsy room. We would have access to a greater range of equipment. I'd like to get a look inside the wounds with a magnifying glass. If you are right about the beast—"

"Of course, I'm right," Evie interrupted.

Joym continued as if he'd not heard her. "—then there might be a chance to find some other clues. Such as how the cuts or gashes were made."

"If it is a beast, then you might think these were from claws," Evie said.

"Quite right. But beasts also bite, do they not?"

Evie nodded. "And there are no signs of bites here. Not unless it only has three huge teeth."

"Exactly so."

"And you don't have a magnifier?"

"No, we only conduct demonstration dissections here. Even so, the porters could bring in such equipment if we

83

decide it's required," he said. He shoved his hand into his pocket and brought out a small leather case. When he opened it, a small lens sat in a brass and leather holder. "I always have this with me for some of the old texts, which are awkward to read. I'm not sure it is much use here."

Evie held out her hand. "May I?"

"Of course."

With the lens in hand, she had to get much closer to the body than she could manage. Joym lowered the gurney a little, which made it a little easier. She started at the topmost gash and stared along the full length of the wound. In truth, she wasn't sure what she was looking for, but she had faith in herself. If something remained to be found, she would find it.

The central gash pierced deeper into the body and had pierced between the ribs to great depth. Near the sternum, the claws –she couldn't see it as being anything else– had notched the bone.

"Oh, wait. Have you seen this?" she asked.

"What?" Joym asked, and he took a few steps closer.

"Looks like dark hair in the wound," she said. "Is that how the body came here, or has it been contaminated since?"

"Let me see." He took the lens from her and selected what looked like a long set of tweezers. "Where?"

Evie pointed.

Joym leaned over the body, lens in one hand and tweezers in the other.

"Maybe you shouldn't get so close," Evie said.

"Nonsense, I have done this many times," he replied.

"But—" she started.

"There. I see it." He reached into the gash and snapped the tips of the tweezers together. He drew out a single dark hair.

"Well?" Evie asked.

He held the strand in the light. "I have no idea what this is. I'll need to look under a microscope. Pass me a slide, please. I put some on the tray."

Evie had never heard of a slide, but she looked into the tray and saw several rectangular pieces of glass. She picked one up. "This?" she asked.

"Perfect, yes." He took the slide and placed the hair on top, then added another piece of glass so the hair could be sandwiched between the two. "It looks quite coarse, but I hope to know more when I look it up."

Evie turned her attention back to the body. The dark glittering seemed strongest around the wounds, particularly the central one where the claws had pierced the soft tissues.

"Do you mind if I take a closer look?" she asked.

"Do whatever you must," he said.

Evie pushed her hand into the central gash, and the soft tissue oozed around her fingers. If she were ever to be sick, this would be the time. She closed her eyes and took a deep breath to steady herself. She called for her gift to rise, to respond to this shadowy infection so she could see with eyes and gift at the same time.

With such close contact, she waited for the touch of the void to reach out and turn her into ice, but it didn't. Although her gift rose on command, she did not yet have full control, and the curse fell away from her, hiding even deeper in the body.

"It's fighting me! How can this accursed body refuse me?" Evie asked. She wouldn't give up.

A hand on her shoulder, followed by the gentle brush of Hesta's gift against her ears, filled her with their conjoined power. She didn't think about why they could be so aligned, or even how, but it worked. Evie made use of that power, the ability to attract to her whatever she wanted. The touch of the curse flowed without resistance into her hands.

Her skin turned red. Not the purple of the void, nor the black of disease and infection, but the colour of freshly spilled blood. The colour was so unnatural and bright that, as she lifted her hands into the light, she thought her skin would drip from her fingers. Instead, the red crept over her hand, over her wrists, and up her arms.

"Evie," Hesta said. "Your hands." She sounded worried.

"It's fascinating," Evie murmured.

Glittering blackness danced over her blood-coloured hands, and then the void rose up in a purple cloud, freezing everywhere it touched her. She closed her eyes as ice gathered on her eyelids and sealed them closed, and her body shivered as more ice burst from her chest.

The next thing she knew, a pair of arms had wrapped around her shoulders and held her in a warm, soft embrace. Even with the chill filling her, she recognised Hesta by touch, by the smell of rosewater and the heat of her skin.

"You shouldn't touch me when I do this," Evie said.

"You've finished," Hesta said. "And I know you would never infect me."

"You don't know that," Evie said. She extracted herself from Hesta's arms. "Thank you for taking care of me, but I can't be sure what I will do. You should not be so quick to risk yourself."

Hesta stared into her eyes. "And if you did, you would heal me." She spoke with such certainty.

Evie sighed. "Yes, you know I would."

"So what is it? What do we face?"

"I don't know." Evie stared at her hands. They were normal now, but under her skin, she saw glittering blackness worming though her body. "But whatever it is, I'm infected."

"Evie, you need to purge it," Hesta said.

"I know, I just needed a moment to look at it more closely."

"Inside of you is more than close enough," Hesta said.

Evie smiled and nodded. She tried to purge right then, but nothing happened. "How odd," she said. The glittering black turned red but didn't react like a disease. It didn't grow and spread; it just sat in her blood. "I can't get rid of this."

"What does that mean?" Joym asked. Evie had almost forgotten he was there.

"It's a curse. Of that I no longer have any doubt. I have no details, and I can't see any more than what I've already seen."

"A curse means it's not a natural disease, then?" he asked.

"Not unless you know of some disease that makes a man split apart." She shook her head. "Maybe I just need to sample more."

"No," Hesta said.

"No? Why not? It causes me no harm."

"You can't know that for sure. Besides I have more experience with curses, and this one scares me." She stepped further away from the gurney. "I can have no part of this. I'll not help you hurt yourself."

Evie knew she was right, but she couldn't ignore the chance to see and know more. Even if the darkness would not come to her without Hesta, there must be more for her to discover.

She brushed her fingers across a particularly ragged portion of the topmost gash. "It seems to me that this is…" Her thoughts faded away.

A surge of blackness raced into her hand, and redness, like blood, covered her hand and burst through her skin. Infection seared through every nerve and the pain took away her breath. She gritted her teeth so hard she thought her jaw would break. Just as quickly, ice rose through her and took the burning away.

She fell to her knees and gasped for breath. She coughed until her chest and throat felt ragged and raw, bringing up tiny shards of ice that landed on the floor and melted in small splatters. She fell to her side and rolled onto her back. She didn't have the energy to sit up, never mind anything else.

Hesta knelt beside her; her expression concerned to the point of terrified. She took Evie's hand in hers and held it in her lap. "Talk to me," she said.

Evie didn't need to look at her hand to know she'd been infected by something. "Apparently I don't need your strength to sponge this fella."

"You did to start. What changed?"

Evie looked at her. "True, I did, but it seems that once you've been touched, the rest is easy."

"I don't like the sound of that. You need to rid yourself of it."

Evie smiled. "I can't. You've touched me and nothing happened."

"Do something. Get rid of it."

"I don't need to. It's not spreading."

"Not yet."

"Well, yes. Not yet." Evie bit her lip. Not yet. At the back of her mind, she remembered the effect of holding on to an infection. How it had grown and almost overwhelmed her. How would she rid herself of the problem this time? By infecting Hesta? She would have to be careful now. "It will be fine. Maybe in the meantime I can get to understand this little bugger."

12

Hesta looked at the people gathered around the table and couldn't help but smile. Afternoon tea with Agatha Hickman, Florie, and Florie's chap, Simple, turned out to be a very pleasant event.

Evie poured tea, but she wore a perpetual frown that had not diminished since they'd examined the body in the Rotunda.

"Are you going to stay with us now?" Agatha asked.

"Maybe. I think it'll be all right," Evie answered. "If I'd been infected by anything it would have shown by now. Hesta would have caught it."

"It's been a week already, and there are no signs of anything like an infection, so I would think it's safe," Hesta said.

"Don't be morbid Evie doesn't get many infections, do you, Evie?" Florie said.

"True enough, but this is different. Besides, I'm here now. If I can pass anything on, I'd have done so by now, so I suppose it doesn't matter where I stay," Evie said.

Hesta shrugged. "Whatever you think best."

Florie pulled her seat closer to Hesta. "Did I tell you the story about Markis?"

"Markis?" It took Hesta a moment to recall her life in the theatre; it seemed like a life time ago. "Strongman Markis?"

Florie giggled. "Yes, him."

"Don't tell me. He was in the middle of a performance and someone lifted one of his heavier weights, but with one hand?"

Florie laughed. "That's the one. Then he draws the loudest heckler in the audience into a lifting competition. But I bet you know how that goes."

"I do. Every once in a while, he does it to keep the audience watching, and a bit of fun keeps them entertained longer."

"Worked, it did," Florie said.

"Do you enjoy being there?" Hesta asked.

"Yes, Miss Estrallia."

"I'm not Estrallia anymore. Just plain old Hesta Bethwood."

"There is nothing plain about a Bethwood," Agatha mumbled.

"Will you not sing for us ever again?" Florie asked.

Hesta looked up to see Evie looking at her. "Maybe one day I might, for the fun of it. But not as a regular thing."

"That's a shame, Miss Bethwood," Simple said.

"Did you go to the theatre, Simon?"

"Call me Simple, like everyone else does," he said. "I did, but I never saw you sing, and Florie does go on so about how fantastic you were."

Hesta chuckled to herself. "Well then, Simple, one day I will return for a performance or two, and I'll make sure you get a seat at the front. Or maybe you would like to be in a private box?"

"Really? That sounds wonderful."

"Of course, I will."

"Now, you two, don't you go bothering Miss Bethwood like that," Agatha said.

"We won't," Florie promised. "Besides, Simple has some news, eh?"

He nodded with such enthusiasm his head bobbed about as though fixed on a spring rather than his spine.

"Go on, tell 'em," Florie urged.

"I've been keeping my ears and eyes open as you asked me before." He looked at Agatha as though he needed permission to speak. "There is a great deal being said at the moment."

Evie stopped what she was doing and sat next to Hesta.

"What did you hear?" Hesta asked.

"Lots of things. Some people say the vitalists have caused demon trouble."

"Do they now, and who are these people?" Evie asked.

He sat upright. "Men at the yard. Some chatter at the pub down by the market, and that place off Willis Street in Cainstown."

"The King George?" Evie asked.

"Aye," Simple said.

"Do they say anything about why vitalists would bring the demons?" Hesta asked.

"To kill the gifted," Florie said.

Simple looked at Florie. "It's a little more than just that." He turned to Hesta. "But she's not wrong. They say the Science of the Father has upset the natural order, and demons have been sent to rid the streets of the gifted."

"That doesn't make sense," Evie said.

"It's what they say," Florie said defensively.

Hesta's thoughts churned through this information. "It doesn't help much, other than to give away the mood of the ordinary people."

"There's more, though," Simple said. "When you listen to a lot of people, the story isn't always the same. Some say that science has upset the balance and it is being used in the name of the Divine Father at the expense of the Divine Mother."

"And that's it?" Evie asked.

Simple shook his head. "They also say that the Divine Mother is very angry at this and she has sent her rage in the form of a beast to cleanse the streets."

"Rage?" Evie asked. "Where did you hear that?"

"A group gathered at the old wife's house," he said. "You know Oklah Wehari?"

"I know her," Evie said.

"A whole crowd gathered in the street one night and—"

"They didn't do anything to her, did they?" Hesta interrupted.

"No, no," Simple said. "They needed help. They know there is something on the streets at night hunting working folk. Many of these people work shifts, see, and it's dangerous on the streets right now."

"It's always dangerous on the streets," Evie said.

"Right enough," he agreed. "Not like this, though." He took a sip of his tea. "They found a man. A dead man near the railway lines. Ripped apart, he was, and—"

"No, don't say it," Florie interrupted.

"Please, do," Hesta said, "but if it is too much for delicate ears, then perhaps we should step into the backyard?"

Simple looked at Agatha, who said, "It's all right. I've heard all sorts of things before."

He swallowed hard. "All right. Something pulled his head clean off and left it on the side. But not before it ate half of him." He looked away. "Do you think they were making it up?"

"I don't know. What did the old wife say?" Hesta asked.

"She's the one what told us all that a beast had come, a cursed beast, to cleanse the streets. We all know that the gifted ones are blessed by our Mother, so they take that to mean we should be looking to keep the gifted safe."

"Well, that's a come around and a half," Evie said.

"That doesn't mean all people welcome the gifted," Hesta said.

"They also say your brother had the right of it," Simple added.

"What about my brother?" Hesta asked.

"That he wanted to make a place in Bristelle for the gifted. Then normal good people would know where to go when things got right upset, like now," he said.

Hesta turned her attention to Evie. "I think now is a good time, don't you?"

"It's always a good time to make things right," Evie replied.

"We are still moving forward with the school," Hesta said. "The Chester-Bethwood Academy. But it would be good if we could gain some kind of legitimacy from the council."

"You could get all the legitimacy you need from the people you help," Agatha said. "You don't need to be looking for more. Not yet at least."

"You are very right, Agatha," Hesta said. "I need to get everything in order right away."

"And I think you need to figure out how to get this beast off the street, no matter what sort of beast it is," Agatha said. "And do it before any good will for the gifted turns into distrust once more."

"I'll do what I can."

"We, Hesta," Evie said. "*We* will do what we can."

13

Afternoon had made way for early evening when Hesta and Evie left Agatha's house. As expected, Charlie waited outside with the calash, ready to take them wherever they wished to go.

Hesta had been quite surprised when Evie had chosen to join her at Bethwood House rather than stay with Agatha and Florie. The small gesture pleased her. She liked the company, as much as anything else.

"Lamplighters are out early," Charlie said, "but I lit the carriage lamps anyway."

Hesta looked along the road to the two gangs who had the task of lighting the streetlights every day. "I used to watch the lamplighter from my window. I've not seen them working in gangs like this, though."

"I know, they usually operate alone," Evie said.

"Indeed, they do."

"Where to? Home, Miss Bethwood?" Charlie asked.

Evie pulled the travel rug over their legs.

"No, not right away, Charlie. I think we need to see the old wife, Oklah Wehari, again. Let's see what she has to say about the current situation," Hesta said.

"Right away, miss.".

"The old wife?" Evie asked as they clattered along Ardmore Street.

"I think so, don't you? If anyone knows anything, she does."

As they made their way, the river of people on the streets dwindled to little more than a trickle. Those who dared the streets rushed by, their shoulders hunched as if they could escape whatever nightmare roamed the shadows.

By the time they reached the heart of Cainstown, the streets were almost deserted. Except for those that gave access to the wise woman's house.

Two braziers sat in the middle of the cobbled lane. The flames reached high above the rims of the metal fire baskets and disgorged sparks and ash into the air. It wasn't that cold, but a dozen or so men gathered around the firepits. When Charlie drove the calash into the street, the group grabbed burning torches and formed a line across the way.

"Let us pass," Charlie shouted.

"Bugger off. No posh nobs 'ere," yelled one.

"Go. Else we'll have to show you what it's like to wear them wheels," added another.

"What do you want me to do, Miss Bethwood?" Charlie asked.

"Wait here." She opened the door to the calash, stepped onto the top step, and then down to the ground. It was always awkward on cobbles, but she made it without a slip and strode toward the men in the street.

"Wait for me," Evie called out.

Hesta stopped halfway between the calash and the men. "Gentlemen, if you would be so good as to stand aside, my friend and I wish to go and see the Old Wife."

The chap at the front, bald and fierce looking, folded his arms across his chest and looked Hesta up and down. "No."

"What the hell's going on?" Evie asked.

"No one passes this way. No one," he said.

Hesta wasn't sure how to get by, not without using her gift. "I wish to see Oklah, the Old Mother. No doubt she expects us."

"No doubt," he said. "But if she expects you, she will tell me so herself."

"Well, damn," Hesta cursed. "Then I'll come back in the morning. Mayhap access to the wise woman will be a little more welcoming."

"You can try," he sneered. Belligerence laced his words. "But don't you go counting on it. Go back where you belong with all them other boss-men types in Salverton."

Evie and Hesta turned away and headed back to the carriage. Hesta hadn't even managed to put her foot on the step when a voice called out loud and clear. "I see you, Hesta Bethwood and Evie Chester. You may come now."

Oklah herself stood in the street. Firelight illuminated the woman, and her white eyes shone with the red and yellow flames of the fires. "Come now. There are things to be said."

The men on the street stood to one side and allowed Evie and Hesta to walk to the house.

"It's a trying time right now," Oklah said.

"You were watching us," Hesta said.

"Yes.".

"I didn't see you," Evie said.

"You must open your eyes better, Evie Chester, if you wish to see all there is to see."

"Such as?" Evie pressed.

"Life, death, and the mysteries of the world around us," Oklah answered.

"And must I be blinded to see as well as you?" Evie asked.

"If it makes you see better, then yes. Blind I may be, but I see all the better for it. You see with your eyes, and yet you fail to see so much. This, I know. Tell me, who is the one who is worse off?"

"I am," Evie said.

"Then there is hope for you."

"When you look at me, what do you see?" Evie asked.

"I see an uncertain woman. Come inside, I have tea ready. There are things we should discuss now."

"Only now?" Hesta asked.

Oklah stared at her with those sightless white eyes, and Hesta shivered.

"Yes, Miss Bethwood. Now is the time," Oklah said.

Inside, the house was exactly as Hesta remembered it. The tea had been made, and there were scones warming on the stovetop. Evie poured the tea, and when she had finished seeing to their needs, sat on a stool near the fireplace.

"Are you cold?" Hesta asked.

"No," Evie replied.

"It is not the cold of the skin that bothers her— it is fear that chills her heart," Oklah said.

"Is it?" Evie asked.

Oklah fiddled with a pale cream disk with the quartered circle of the Old Wife at her throat and nodded. "The fear in your heart is as clear to me as the colours of your clothing are to you. And that fear is a dark glimmer that has found and settled within you. It is like a pulse of other life."

Evie looked up sharply. "You can see it?"

"I told you, there are things best seen without eyes."

She inclined her head to one side and regarded Hesta with an unnerving sightless stare. "And you are also different."

"Am I?" Hesta said.

"Hesta Bethwood, you have a rosy glow to your soul, and I like this in you."

"You can see changes in my soul?" Hesta asked. She didn't need Oklah to know that there had been many recent changes in her life. She was no longer cursed for a start, and although Godwyn had died, she no longer had any dubious business practices hanging over her head. On top of that, she had Evie.

Oklah didn't answer her question. She sipped at her tea until she'd drunk it all, then held the cup out to Evie. "More tea, with a little more sweetness, if you will. These old bones need it."

"You were expecting us," Hesta said. "You knew we would come."

"Of course. Did you think it would be any other way?" Oklah countered.

"Never mind. I could do with answers, not riddles," Evie said. She handed Oklah a fresh tea. "There is so much I need to know, and if I don't understand soon, I think it will be the death of me."

"You are right. The death of you, the death of Hesta, and the bloody death of many people in this city," Oklah said.

"Well, that's encouraging," Hesta said.

"Don't be so flippant in the face of such great danger, Hesta Bethwood," Oklah admonished.

Hesta stared at the fire for a moment before she turned back to the old woman. "Forgive me, Old Wife. Much has happened of late, and we are caught in the midst of great upset and sadness."

"I was sorry to hear about your brother," Oklah said, her voice soft.

"Thank you. We seem to be caught up in some greater mystery that we can't see or understand."

"You are."

"We need your help to understand these things," Hesta said.

"Much better," Oklah said. She sipped her tea. "You have found a way to join your gifts together." It wasn't a question.

"Yes. Sometimes. At least a little."

"She gives me strength to do things I might not manage on my own," Evie said.

"I know. Now that you have started, you must get better at it."

"How?" Evie asked.

"First, a warning. The more you work together, the more you will attract that which you find least attractive. The stronger you are, the worse it will get."

"So what's the point in getting stronger if everything gets worse?" Evie asked.

"Impatience is not one of the virtues, Evie Chester. You must remember that," Oklah said.

Evie held up her hands in surrender.

"Just so," Oklah muttered, and sipped her tea.

It occurred to Hesta, as they sat there, that Oklah was observing them over the rim of her cup. She couldn't be sure, though, and those white eyes gave nothing away. If anything, the thought that she might be under scrutiny filled her with doubt and uncertainty.

Oklah coughed to clear her throat and handed her cup to Evie. "Very well. This is what I know. You cannot have a siren and a syphon in the same space without calling attention to that place."

"You mean Bristelle?" Evie asked.

"Just so," Oklah agreed. "But you have even more plans, an academy of sorts. When it is created and word gets around, you will attract the gifted, which is what you wish."

Hesta nodded.

"When you all gather together and make your place in this world, it will attract even more attention from…from those who wish you harm. This is the price you must pay," Oklah said.

"Are you saying this is a bad thing, and we shouldn't go ahead with it?" Hesta asked.

"We are not here to discuss my opinion on the matter," Oklah said. "The will is your own. The question is, do you still think you should?"

"Because we will face more difficulties?" Evie asked.

Oklah didn't answer.

"I will do what I think is right, no matter how much hardship it brings to me," Hesta said. "And I hope Evie will stand with me in this matter."

"I do, and I will," Evie replied.

"It is good that you know your own minds. But you must also know that hardship will follow. It may even bring harm to those people you wish to help," Oklah said.

"There is always hardship when a person is gifted, but we will do whatever we can to keep them safe," Hesta said.

"Or we will find a safe place for them," Evie added. She looked at Hesta, and they nodded to each other.

"That is what we will do." Hesta turned her attention to Oklah. "It is decided. We help those who need us, no matter the cost."

"Good. Because the times ahead will be hard for you. Hard for you both," Oklah said. "The demon was but a small measure of the force that—"

"You know about the demon?" Hesta interrupted. "How?"

Oklah's drawn out, exaggerated sigh emphasized a degree of frustration with the question. "I know. In the same way that I see without seeing, I know things. Sometimes I get to see the mysteries of the world, no matter how strange. But always, everything I know is because the Great Mother wills it so."

"Of course, Old Mother," Hesta said, and she looked down at the floor. "Forgive my impertinence."

Oklah laughed. "There is nothing to forgive. Remember that I am not our Mother at all. I am an Old Wife, and a poor echo of the will of the divine spirit. It shows great respect to be called Old Mother, thank you, but never confuse me with the great one herself."

"And what does she say about the beast that hunts the city?" Evie asked. "Where can we find it?"

She and Hesta stared at Oklah and waited for her wisdom. Her eyes turned a glowing shade of silver. "You don't hunt the beast. It will hunt you," she said. "It has hunted in this city for many moons, but its prey rarely makes it to the attention of the public." She turned her head to face Evie. "You carry its dark touch, the mark of the cursed one. It will try to make you a part of itself, or take back what has been shared."

"It's coming for me?" Evie asked.

"Yes."

"How will it find me?"

"It will follow your scent, once it has identified you. For now, it knows that another is marked, and the curse calls to this beast. You know that already."

"I suspected as much," Evie answered.

"But that is not the true problem for you, is it?"

Evie shook her head.

"What's going on? Am I missing something?" Hesta asked.

"I can't purge," Evie whispered.

"Yes, you can," Hesta said. "When you are more full, you can purge into me. You've done that before."

Evie stood up and shuffled to the front door.

"Evie?"

Evie stopped, and when she answered, she spoke so quietly that Hesta could barely hear her. "No, I can't. You've already touched me, and that didn't trigger the purge. But when I get more, I might not be able to control it, and when I purge, it'll kill you. Or take away your voice, or something."

"You don't know that."

"Evie has figured out how this curse works," Oklah said.

"She has? How?"

"Tell her, Old Mother. I can't." Evie opened the front door and let it slam behind her.

Hesta sat, shocked as well as concerned at Evie's departure. "What's going on?"

Oklah sighed. She sounded tired, and she looked worse. "She can't control the curse. She senses it within her, waiting. Sometimes it rises like a fire of rage and calls out to her."

"Why did she not say anything?"

"She doesn't want to face it just yet. She fears she will succumb to the curse herself. If that happens, then she will become a beast and kill like the other. Together they would spread this curse through the city and bathe everyone in blood."

Hesta shivered. "We'll stop it."

"She fears that if she purges into anyone else, even if they survive, they will become a target for the beast. Would you pay that price?"

Hesta didn't have to think of her answer. "Yes."

"Maybe she wouldn't want you to pay," Oklah said.

"What should I do to help her?"

"Do what you can. Do what you think is right."

"Will Evie be all right?"

"I don't know, but there is one thing I can tell you. To kill the beast, someone has to die, I just don't know who. You should both ready yourself for that."

"In case?"

Oklah nodded.

"I'll get my affairs in order."

"I didn't say it would be you who has to die."

"And I'm saying it won't be Evie. No matter what."

"Hesta Bethwood, now I understand the rosy glow to your soul."

14

E vie slumped into the seat of the calash and stared at the fires bursting out of the braziers.

"Is everything all right, miss?" Charlie asked.

"Call me Evie, Charlie. I'm no miss anything."

"As you like," he said.

"And no, there's nothing wrong. Tired is all."

"Will Miss Bethwood be long?"

"I don't know."

"Excuse me if I'm speaking out of turn, but a visit with the Old Wife is always disconcerting," Charlie said.

Evie tore her gaze from the flames and turned her attention to Charlie. It took a moment for her eyes to adjust to the darkness. "I know. And it gets worse every time you see her."

"Ain't that the truth," he said.

"Have you been to her?"

"Aye, me and the wife had an issue or two."

"Did she help?"

He shrugged. "We'll know within the year, I guess."

"Good luck to you, then," Evie said.

"Thanks, miss." He pointed. "Miss Bethwood is on her way back, looks like."

Evie watched Hesta as she strolled slowly along the street. She didn't seem to be paying much attention to her surrounding, or the men around her. Evie opened the door and stepped out to meet her. "Hesta?" she called. "Is everything all right?"

Hesta stopped dead in her tracks, but when she looked up, she smiled. "Be right there. Just thinking."

Evie leaned against the side of the calash and waited for her. "What did she say? Did she tell you everything?"

"I think we should talk about this over something strong and numbing." She climbed into the carriage with Evie, waited until they'd settled in, and then banged her hand against the carriage door. "Home Charlie. Then you should retire for the evening. I think we'll have a full day on the morrow."

"Yes, ma'am."

Evie said no more as they drove to Bethwood House. Even when they were inside, she said nothing except to arrange for a pot of tea and a decanter of brandy, which she had Mrs Dunn serve in the library rather than the drawing room or the parlour.

Hesta drank two glasses of the fiery liquid before she would speak. Evie sipped her tea and left the spirits for later.

"So?" Evie prompted.

Hesta finished her drink and poured another. She swallowed half of that one with a grimace. She took a deep breath and then spoke in a rush, as though she were afraid that if she didn't get them all out at once, she wouldn't get them out at all. "Oklah is sure one of us will die, and I don't want it to be you. Why didn't you tell me you couldn't purge?"

"Hesta—"

"Why don't you tell me these things? Don't you trust me? Don't you care what I think? Do you think I don't care?"

Evie reached over and stopped Hesta from taking another drink. "I did tell you."

"No. I would have remembered if you'd said it was going to hurt you."

Evie stroked the side of Hesta's hand with her thumb. "I said I couldn't purge after I touched the body."

"But you wouldn't have been infected without my help. I made you sponge."

"Listen, it's not your fault. I just can't purge. I can't get a handle on it at all."

"But you made it sound like it was nothing more than normal. Why didn't you say?" Hesta asked.

"I would have, but I really didn't know. Until after we touched."

Hesta stared at her. "What does that mean?"

Evie sat back in her seat. "When there is something I can't figure out, or when I don't purge in time, then the moment I touch someone, I disgorge all sickness into them, whether I want to or not. I used to think it happened only when I was full. Now, I'm not so sure." Evie sipped her brandy. It burned her mouth, and when she swallowed, the burning followed all the way down and settled like acid in her gut. "I've been infected a while. Usually that means the infection is getting more concentrated, and if I touch someone, I would spread something far worse than what I took. Worse, if I don't cleanse myself, then I get sick. And I can't cleanse, Hesta. Even after all the lessons I learned as a result of Godwyn's efforts to make me his weapon, I can't do anything."

"We'll work it out," Hesta said.

"Did the Old Wife tell you I might become the beast?"

"She did, but we don't know that for sure."

"What if I do succumb? What if I become a raging beast?" Evie asked.

"Oklah said we can kill the beast."

"And the price to pay?"

"I will pay that price. Promise me you will offer me as the cost of this?"

"I can't!" Evie said, horrified that she would have to make the choice.

"To save the city and everyone in it, you must."

"No."

Hesta rose from her seat and knelt before Evie. "Promise me, Evie. Promise me that you will kill the beast, and that you will do what you can to save yourself. You can make more of a difference to the people than I can. You can heal them, and that makes you too valuable to lose."

Evie shook her head from side to side. "I promised myself that I would never choose to cause the death of anyone again. Don't make me do it."

"You must do whatever it takes to stop this."

15

E vie woke early. It still seemed odd to be in a Bethwood house and have neither chains nor restraints. Better yet: here, she would be fed and cared for. To make sure nothing had changed, she made her way to the kitchen.

Mrs Dunn had already started her work day when she walked in, and the kitchen was warm and welcoming.

"Good morning, Miss Chester. What would you like for your breakfast?"

"Tea would be good, if there's any."

"Not yet, but the water's almost ready to make a pot."

Evie yawned. "I have no idea why, but every time I walk into this kitchen, I feel sleepy."

Mrs Dunn smiled broadly. "It's because I work hard to keep it comfortable, and the smell of cooking always settles the heart and soul."

"Must be that," Evie agreed. "And please call me Evie, not Miss Chester. That makes me feel odd. I'm just me. Evie."

"Oh, I couldn't do that," Mrs Dunn said. "It would be improper."

"Then how about when I'm in the kitchen and no one else is around, you call me Evie."

"That would be lovely, Evie. I'm Innie Dunn, so call me Innie, if you like."

"Thank you, Innie."

"Now, what would you like to eat? Miss Bethwood insists we feed you up, and I wouldn't like to be remiss in my duties."

"Hot toast and jam," Evie said. She didn't even have to think about it. Mrs Dunn cut the bread a good half inch thick, put a slice on the toasting fork and put rested it in front of the glowing coals of the cooking range. When done, she smothered the toasted bread with butter and a thick layer of jam. Evie's mouth watered at the sight of it.

"Tonight, I'm making a big game pie. Will you be dining here with Miss Bethwood?"

"If you are making a pie, how can I refuse? I'll tell Hesta I'm staying for dinner, at least."

Mrs Dunn grinned. "In that case, I'll also make a mound of buttered potatoes and a thick gravy. How's that sound?"

"Perfect," Evie said. "I get so spoiled here, it is no wonder I never go home."

The door opened.

"Good morning, Miss Bethwood," Mrs Dunn said. "Evie, I mean, Miss Chester is going to stay for dinner again."

Hesta chuckled. "Yes. I also heard that the only reason she stays is so she might enjoy your cooking."

"Hesta—" Evie started.

"It's a good reason, mind. But I think that puts me in my place, don't you?"

"There's no way to answer that," Evie said.

"It would probably be best to say nothing, then," Hesta said. She grinned with amusement, and her smile not only lit up her face, but the whole kitchen at the same time.

"Tea, Miss Bethwood?" Mrs Dunn asked.

"Yes, please, and the usual breakfast."

"Coming right up."

"Any plans today, Evie?" Hesta asked.

"Not really. I'm still not allowed back into the hospital, and in the current situation, it's probably wise to avoid infections."

"Would you like to spend the day with me? It's not an exciting day, but I do need to inspect my properties and clarify what I have and what I need. Most important, after I've looked at the properties, I need to see Mr Grobber to find out what news he has for me."

"If you are going to see him, then I couldn't let you go without an escort," Evie said.

"I can look after—"

"I'm sure you can," Evie interrupted. "But yes, I'll go with you."

"Then we'll have a fine day. I look forward to it."

Mrs Dunn made a large pot of tea and let it stand on the table. "That reminds me, Charlie put the morning paper on the hallway table for you. We weren't sure whether you wanted to read it in the parlour or in the library."

"Thank you." Hesta said. "Where do you prefer, Evie?"

"I like it here or in the library," Evie said.

"Then we'll stay here. I'll just get the paper."

It didn't take Hesta long, but when she returned to the kitchen, her face did not display her earlier good cheer.

"What's wrong?" Evie asked.

Hesta threw the newspaper on the table. "Another beast attack. The papers say they're getting more frequent and more violent."

"*More* violent?"

"Yes." Hesta grabbed the paper and folded it over so the headlines didn't show. "I think my plans for today have just changed. The houses will have to wait. Our first call must be to Mr Grobber."

"Then I'd better not eat too much. That man turns my stomach," Evie said.

"They all turn your stomach," Hesta said.

Evie poured out two cups of tea. "Well, yes, but I think that's to be expected, don't you?"

Hesta picked up her cup, but she stared into the dark tea with a thoughtful expression. "Yes. Given the circumstances, I think it is very reasonable."

Evie nodded. They did not need to speak more about such things. They both knew her past.

They were so focussed on each other that when Innie placed a plate of toast in front of her, Evie flinched in her seat. She clutched her throat in exaggerated shock. "You fair made me jump there, Mrs Dunn."

"Daydreaming, you were," Innie answered. "Now, eat it up, and if you want any more, just say so."

Evie took a look at the two thick slices of toast. Butter melted over the edges of the crust, and Innie had put a large bowl of strawberry preserves before her. She grabbed the spoon and put a huge dollop of jam on her toast. Her mouth watered at the thought of the hot toast and all of that buttery sweetness.

"Eat up," Hesta urged. "As soon as you're ready, we'll get Charlie to take us out. And if you're lucky, I'll let you treat me to lunch."

Evie snorted. "My choice of venue, then."

"Very well. But I draw the line at eating whelks whilst standing at the dockside."

Evie laughed. "I'll think of some place with chairs."

Charlie, with the calash and horse ready, waited for them at the curbside when they left the house. "Where to, Miss Bethwood?"

"Blest Hill, please, Charlie. I need to visit Mr Grobber."

"Right away," he answered.

16

C harlie drove them around to the back of the house in Blest Hill. Evie shuddered as they drove through the gates into the courtyard. She had so many memories of this place, and few of them were good.

Around the gate and the courtyard, quite a few people had congregated in small groups. They were beggar gangs for the most part, and although Evie couldn't identify any one person or group, she recognised the slouch and stare of people who lived in the shadows of the street. These were the sort of people who'd hunted her when she'd escaped Godwyn Bethwood the first time.

Evie shivered, barely able to control the fear that rose inside her chest and squeezed her heart.

Mr Wiggins strode across the yard to meet them, and Evie wanted to sink into the upholstery where no one could see her. Hesta reached out and grabbed her hand.

"It's all right. I'm here, and no one will harm you," she whispered.

"Good morning, miss," Mr Wiggins said. He froze when he saw Evie. "You? What the hell are—"

"You know who I am," Hesta interrupted.

"Yes," he replied.

"Good. Since Evie is my friend and business partner. You will accord her the greatest respect."

"Yes miss Bethwood."

"Then I'm here to see Mr Grobber. Is he here?"

He took a step backwards. "Yes, Miss Bethwood, he's inside. We've been told to expect you."

"Good. Show us the way."

"Yes, miss."

Mr Grobber sat at the kitchen table with his feet on one of the chairs.

"Visitors," Mr Wiggins said. He stepped to one side so Hesta could follow him in.

The chairs grated across the flagstone floor as Grobber jumped to his feet. "Miss Bethwood, Miss Chester. Good to see you. Take a seat." He made a show of cleaning off the chairs before they sat.

Evie sat, but Hesta stood behind her, her hand on Evie's shoulder.

"Wiggins, go get Finn, Farik, and Fallow," Grobber said.

"What strange names," Hesta said.

"They're the kings of the three beggar gangs. We were still negotiating business," he said.

"And what were their demands?" Hesta asked.

"They want one schilling for each king and one copper a week for each of the gang members," he said. "They're thieving scum and need a kick up the arse to put 'em in their place."

"Violence is not always the answer. Let's see what they have to say," Hesta said.

When the beggar kings joined them, Evie was shocked to discover the leaders were no more than boys themselves. One of them may have been Florie's age, if that. They each had dark hair, grubby complexions, and the insolence born of a hard life. She knew that look.

"Finn, Farik, and Fallow," Grobber introduced them, pointing to each in turn.

"You're all younger than I expected," Hesta said.

"Yes, miss. When we get too old, we can't do what we do."

"Finn, is it?" Hesta asked.

He nodded his reply.

"What is it that you do?"

He sniffed and wiped his nose along his sleeve. "We beg. We find stuff out, we nick stuff, and we find things." He chinned towards Evie. "We find folks who dunna wanna be found."

Evie let her eyes close for a moment and took a few deep breaths. Hesta squeezed her shoulder and that was enough to melt the ice of fear that clutched at her heart.

"And what happens when you get too old or too big?" Hesta asked.

"We get with another gang and find a skill to fit," Finn replied.

"I see," she said. "What if I could give you other options?"

"Hey, miss, I'm Farik, and when we gets freedom, we don't need no do-gooders nor reformers to be interfering."

"I understand," Hesta said.

"So, lady, what's the deal?" Fallow asked.

"Information," Hesta replied.

"We told ya the rates," Finn said.

"You ask too much," Grobber interrupted. "That's daylight robbery."

"How much d'ya wanna know stuff?" Farik asked. "If you wanna know, you'll pay."

"How many are in each gang?" Evie asked.

Finn shrugged. "A lot."

"Maybe ten in each gang," Grobber said.

"That's a great deal of money for no discernible gain, as far as I can see," Hesta said.

"Take it or leave it," Fallow said. "You heard Farrow, like, you want it you pay for it."

"So far, you want us to pay, but you're not promising to deliver," Hesta said.

'Hesta, forgive me talking like this, but Finn has a big sore on his back and it's infected. Maybe a health trade if needed?' Evie said directly to Hesta's mind.

'Thank you,' Hesta replied. Aloud, she said. "Our discussion doesn't seem to be getting us very far. Maybe we have to think in a different way."

Finn looked at them through narrowed eyes. "I don't think so, lady."

"Let's start at the beginning, shall we? I'm not sure what Mr Grobber has told you yet."

"I've only mentioned the basics at this point," Mr Grobber replied. "I thought I would leave the specifics to you."

"Good," Hesta said. "We are setting up the Chester-Bethwood Academy, and—"

"We ain't interested in no learning places," Farik said.

"Oh, this is not a school," Hesta continued. "This is a placed for the gifted. A safe place for us. And a place where our unique skills may be put to good use."

Finn snorted. "You're laughing, ain't yah."

"Deadly serious," Hesta said.

"Finn," Evie said, "I have a gift, and I know there is a huge sore on your back. I can see it. It must hurt like hell, and yet you can't get anyone to look at it."

"What the frick are you on about?" Finn said.

"You know," Fallow nudged him in the side. "We all seen it."

"I can make it go away," Evie said.

"Bollocks."

"It's true, Finn. You show Miss Chester where it hurts, and she'll make it better," Mr Grobber said.

'Are you sure?' Hesta asked Evie.

Evie stood up. "Take your shirt off and show me your back."

Finn pulled his shoulders back and held himself stiff.

"If my magic is good enough for the lords and posh nobs of the city, I think it'll be all right for you," Evie said.

"I'm no toff."

"Sick is sick, no matter who you are. But you've got summat infected on your back, which is simple." She smiled. "And for me, this is a whole lot more wholesome than making sure Lord Wotnot's tadger don't fall off."

Finn snickered.

"So?" Evie prompted.

"Good enough for them, good enough for me." He didn't bother unbuttoning his shirt, just lifted it in one and slid it over his head. When he turned around, Evie's gift flared at the sight of the infection. His friends, Farik and Fallow, stepped away, as though now that they could see the sickness, they didn't wish to catch it.

The source of the original problem was minor, or rather it hadn't been much to worry about at the time. Now, though, a pus-filled eruption held court in a mass of purple, inflamed skin. Lines of dark contamination stretched out, and if she didn't do something, she knew the injury would shorten his life.

"What happened? Catch yourself on a nail?"

"Broken glass," he said.

"Yes, that would do it. The cut brought sickness into the skin."

"Can you fix it?" he asked. For just a moment, the boy he should have been shone through the tough bravado of a beggar king.

Evie let her gift sift through the sickness. "Yes," she said. She looked at Hesta. *'Hesta, I need your strength. My skill is weakened.'*

Hesta stood at Evie's side and rested a reassuring hand on

her shoulder. The touch of the Siren's gift brushed against Evie's ears as Hesta hummed what seemed a simple tune but was anything but simple.

Strength flowed through her, and as her palms touched Finn's back, the sickness flowed from him into her hands. Her fingers turned yellow, with veins of red and purple. The infection rose through her fingers and didn't take long to settle completely into her bloodstream.

She pulled away when she was done. The glass cut looked red now, normal. "I need a bandage—something clean—and if you have any antiseptic, that would be helpful."

"We don't have anything like that," Grobber said.

Evie sighed. "All right. I can't do any more for now. Except give you some advice. You know the Old Wife in Cainstown?"

"I know the witch," Finn answered. "But we don't mess with witches. Not when they control your head." He tapped the side of his head to demonstrate.

"Even when they make you better?" Evie asked.

He shrugged. "Fair point. But that don't mean we can trust them."

"By witches you mean the gifted ones?"

"Yeah, them. Witches."

"You can trust Oklah Wehari. She knows her herbs and all the old lore . Go to her, ask her to make a salve for your back and tell her I'll pay if you don't have the money."

"I can pay my own way."

"All right. Get dressed. And after we're done you must see her, otherwise the healing will be for nothing. Hear me?"

"I hear you," he answered.

"Do you need to do your thing in private?" Grobber asked.

Evie waved him off. "Later. I think we need to conclude this business first."

Finn looked at Farik and Fallow. They didn't say anything,

but they nodded. "What do you want and what are you offering?"

"You know who and what we are. Did Mr Grobber discuss any of our specific needs with you?" Hesta asked.

"Naw, like he said. The basics. He just said you would pay for information on a regular basis, like."

"Quite right, too. I will. But it's not any old information. I need you to look for specific things."

"Right, yeah." He sniffed and wiped his nose on the back of his hand. "Since we done the healing of me and all that, that makes us associates."

Hesta nodded.

"We were right sorrowed to hear about your brother. Him being a reformist and that."

"A reformist?" Evie asked. "Godwyn Bethwood a reformist?"

"Yeah," Finn said. "He was all for looking after the gifted with reforms and things."

"Yes, my brother was a good man," Hesta said.

"Yeah, right. With all due respect and that, the Bethwood I knew would as soon cut your throat as be seen as any do-gooder," Evie said.

"No," Hesta said, and shook her head emphatically. "No. He was not like that."

Finn shrugged. "Don't matter to me, like. Me and the boys reckoned that some witch, a gifted one, made his mind bend, see. And if they can bend him, they can bend anyone."

"What if he just discovered the error of his ways?"

"Then I'm the King of the Angles," Finn said.

"He changed for good reason," Evie said. She turned to Grobber. "Tell them, Mr Grobber. Tell them who I am and what I was to Godwyn."

"This is Evie Chester. She was a slave to Bethwood. He kept her chained in the stables outside and used her to get money and favours from the most powerful in the city."

Finn stared at her. "But you don't got slave marks."

"Oh, believe me, she was marked and branded many times," Grobber said. "But they never stuck."

"I have a friend. About your age. We were slaves together," Evie said. "She makes fire at the ends of her fingers and can make a cup of cold water hot."

"Florie," Finn said.

"You know her?" Evie asked.

"Simple's girl, ain't she? She's all right," he said.

Evie chuckled to herself at how easy it was to distrust a group but not an individual, not once they got to know that person.

"We're trying to make it so no one becomes a slave like me, or Florie, and we need a place to be ourselves."

"Sounds fair," Finn said. "What do you need us for?"

"Two things. We want to know about gifted people who are in hiding. Or making their gift hidden. Some of them might not be good people and some might be good people who need us. We want to know about them," Hesta said.

"We can do that. And would ya like to know about them that claim to be gifted but ain't?"

"I would, yes."

"We can do that as well," Finn said. "Anything else?"

"The beastly murders," Hesta said.

"We need to know as much as we can if we have any hope of catching it," Evie said.

The three boys faced each other, and although they didn't actually speak, they moved their hands and their bodies.

'Hesta, they do that hand speak,' Evie said. It didn't occur to her to wonder how she could use the mind-speak with so little effort.

'I know, I'm watching,' Hesta replied. After a few moments, Hesta clapped her hands together and gestured to the boys.

Farik's eyes grew wide.

"You know?" Finn asked aloud.

Hesta stopped moving her hands. "I do. I taught Godwyn. But Evie doesn't."

Finn looked at Hesta and then at Evie. "Whatever they tell you about the murderer, it's probably lies. It's been going on for a while. Every month, there are bodies in the shadows, and the constables make them disappear."

"Disappear?" Evie asked.

"Well, not like magic and such, but they take the remains and burn 'em outta the way before they're seen." He shrugged. "But the killings are more often now, more than once a month."

"I feared as much. It seemed odd that so many deaths would suddenly appear without any kind of clue as to who caused it." Hesta said.

"Gets worse. Friend of ours is a bit bent, see, like your Florie. Sparky, we calls him. He don't have much skill, like, but he's one of us. We trust and care for our own, see, no matter what. Anyways, Sparky was down the lanes towards Ardmore when he saw it."

"Saw what?" Evie asked.

"The beast. All furry with a big mouth. Eight feet tall, if not more. And it near jumped over one of the walls in one bound. Its claws were huge and sparked like a dynamo gone mad, like. Scared Sparky shitless, it did."

Grobber snorted. "I think Sparky has been out in the sun too long, mate."

Finn fisted his hands and rested them on his hips. "And that's why we don't talk to you people."

"I believe you," Evie whispered.

"You do?" Finn asked. He sounded surprised.

"I do, too," Hesta added.

He looked at them through eyes narrowed with suspicion. "Do you truly?"

Evie nodded her head. "I've started training to be a nurse up at the hospital, and there was a body."

Finn nodded.

"I found a long black hair on the dead man, but it didn't look like any animal hair I've ever seen. They are trying to work it out now, but I don't think they'll get anywhere. What do you say?"

Finn unclenched his hands and let them fall to his sides. "I think Sparky can exaggerate a little like the best of us, but I know the wall he mentioned and nothing ordinary could jump that."

"We need to know where and when the beast appears," Hesta said. "Can you find that out without putting any of your gangs at risk?"

Finn cocked his head to one side. "Who cares if one of the beggar gangs die?"

"I care," Hesta said.

"I care as well," Evie added.

"Evie and I would like to take out this beast, for the good of the city and the people in it. But we can't do much if we miss it. The beast kills and then hides away. We have to get closer."

The three boys gestured to each other until they made a decision, and Finn spoke for them. "We'll find it for you. And we'll be ears and eyes for you. A sixpence apiece for each gang each week, and we'll use all the street folk. No extra charge. But a bonus when the news is useful would be good for us. That's fair."

Hesta nodded. "Very fair." She reached into a small purse attached inside her skirt and flipped a silver schilling at the boys. "An advance and thank you for being here. As well as what we've discussed, all Bethwood properties, Godwyn's and mine, including the academy at Bethwood House are protected from unwanted attentions."

Finn grinned. "I'll get yer houses marked up as safe, Miss Bethwood. And we'll send runners to your house to keep you apprised of the situation."

"Fancy words, Finn," Evie said.

"Learned from the best," he answered. "The sooner that beast is gone, the safer normal people can be again. But if you wanna know where to start looking, I'd focus on the lanes at the back of Ardmore. That's where it all started, if you ask me."

"Do you think so?" Evie asked. "I have friends in Ardmore."

"The first of the bodies found its way there. And the second," he said.

"What about the more recent ones?" Hesta asked.

"They were closer to Cainstown," he said. "At least one was close to Badesville, but it always seems to circle back to Ardmore."

"Then we'll start in Ardmore," Evie said.

17

Hesta stood on the road outside Godwyn's former residence in the Queens Park district. The Crescent was comprised of a curved terrace of conjoined town houses. Four storeys high, they appeared almost identical: huge, with a pale stone frontage, and black iron railings. Number fourteen, her new house, stood towards the northern end of the crescent and faced the open parkland.

Evie stood at her side and whistled. "What a house!"

"Isn't it just," Hesta agreed.

"You look surprised. You have been here before, haven't you?"

"Once," Hesta answered. "I know that seems odd, but either I was at the theatre, or Godwyn was busy working."

"I see," Evie said.

"Most of all, I spent years feeling sorry for myself. Every time he invited me, I refused."

"Why? He was your brother, and you were important to each other."

"Because company, and dinner parties in particular, are quite challenging when you can't speak." Hesta snorted. "That is an understatement, of course."

"Why is that?" Evie asked. She looked worried, though.

"When you can't speak, people think you're deaf and simple. So they shout, as though the force of their own words will lend a voice to a ravaged throat."

Hesta looked down when Evie grabbed her hand and squeezed.

"I was amazed by that hand-talking thing. It's so clever."

Hesta couldn't stop laughter from escaping then. "It didn't seem so clever when we were learning. It took us years to say anything meaningful. Then when Godwyn found a healer who could help me, we'd rush through practicing it with sounds until my voice gave out again. Over time, we grew better at the silent talking. I think it kept me sane."

"Now you're better, and I get to drive you mad instead."

"Yes," Hesta said. She crossed the road to the green in front of the houses. The green lawn looked perfect and well maintained. Ornamental trees surrounded the benches set around a small ornamental pond. The trees had been pruned and looked well kept; mulch covered the roots but had been contained with circles of pretty stones.

Flower beds, filled with flowers and not a single weed, burst with colour. Hesta took a deep breath and filled her nose with the scent of the flowers. "It's so beautiful here," she said.

She turned back to the houses. Identical pathways in pale and well-maintained stone passed through the wrought iron gates to each house entrance.

"Ready?" Evie asked.

"As I can be. I wonder what it will be like inside. It's been a long while," Hesta said.

"No idea, but I bet it will look expensive."

Hesta hooked her arm through Evie's. "Let's go, then."

Even though she had the key to the front door, it didn't feel right to use it. She held the key out like a dagger, ready to do battle. "It feels strange going into his home when he's not there," Hesta said.

"It's your house now. He gave it to you."

She stared at the key a moment longer and then inserted the round barrel into the lock and turned it. The mechanism clunked and unlocked. She pushed the door open and, from the threshold, stared into the huge hallway.

As soon as she stepped inside, a man in a black suit strode into the foyer from the other end. He stood tall and stiff, as though he would rather break than bend. He had the brown eyes and dark hair common in Bristelle, although grey peppered the sides of his temples and made him look almost distinguished. "Excuse me, are you expected?" he asked.

Unless her brother had found a way to invite guests whilst he lay in his grave, the chap before them was trying to maintain some semblance of normalcy. She had met this man before, even if he didn't recognise her.

"Expected? I should think so. I'm Hesta, Hesta Bethwood, and this was my brother's house."

He removed a set of spectacles from his inside pocket and put them on. "Great Mother of us all, forgive me, Miss Bethwood. Without my glasses, things can be a little less sharp than they should be." The man bowed low and respectfully in her direction. "My condolences on your loss, Miss Bethwood. We have been anticipating your visit. Please, come in. Can I take your coats?"

Hesta slipped off her jacket and held it out for him to take. "You'll have to—" She stopped where she stood and slapped her head. "Forgive me, you must be John Hobart. Pleased to meet you, Mr Hobart. So much has happened of late that I really have forgotten the common courtesies."

"Yes, Miss Bethwood. It is to be expected, I think."

"Still, there is no room for rudeness, and it must have been a worry when no one came after the untimely death of my brother."

"Yes, miss."

"Especially as your wife and daughter are also here under my brother's employ," Hesta continued.

"We did wonder. Although we did have a visit from your brother's legal representative to let us know about the change in circumstances, but we were concerned when no one came to see us."

"Let me allay your fears as much as I can. I have not decided what will happen with this property, but you will be provided for."

John looked relieved. "Thank you, miss. Mrs Hobart will be relieved. It is not easy to find a good position at our age."

"I should like to meet her," Hesta said. "But shall we be informal and do so in the kitchen?"

"As you wish," he answered, and led the way to the rear of the house.

Along the hallway, there were several closed doors. It would have been nice to wander around and discover the house for herself, but that would have to wait until after she'd been introduced. After all, the staff needed to meet their new mistress, and they would need to be introduced to Evie, too.

Mr Hobart pushed open a door near the back of the house and stepped through to keep the door open for Hesta.

"John, who was at the door?" a feminine voice asked from inside the kitchen.

Hesta strode into the room with Evie at her side.

"Miss Bethwood, this is my wife, Ivy," Mr Hobart said. "She takes care of the cooking and other such details."

Mrs Hobart, of stout proportions and wearing a flour-covered apron, managed a clumsy curtsy.

"Hello, Mrs Hobart, I'm Hesta Bethwood. Please, there is no need for such a formal greeting."

"Thank you, Miss Bethwood. Please, call me Ivy."

"And this is my good friend and companion Evie Chester. She is as much a part of my family as Godwyn."

"Of course, Miss Bethwood," Ivy answered. "Can I get you anything?"

"Tea would be lovely," Hesta answered. "I understand there are others here?"

"My daughter, Maisie, helps out as a maid, and there is young Jack who does the odd jobs."

"Are they here?"

"They're at school," John Hobart said.

Hesta had thought their daughter had reached her majority. "Your daughter is at school?" she asked.

"Yes, ma'am. When her duties here are done, she helps out at the school near the docks. That's where Jack goes."

"Is she a school teacher?" Hesta asked.

"Oh, no. She copies out sections from books so the kids can take those words home with them."

"She writes out words for others."

"Yes, ma'am."

"How wonderful," Hesta said.

"And also, when Maisie goes to school, she can make sure Jack does, too."

"Oh, I understand. That's excellent. I hope to meet them both later." Hesta turned to John. "But a tour of the house would be in order first, I think, so I can familiarise myself with the whole house."

18

Hesta sat in a rather comfortable leather captain's chair next to Godwyn's desk, an oversized mahogany monstrosity that dominated the whole of the study. Although immaculate, the green leather writing surface looked well used. Evie sat on an occasional seat next to an escritoire in the corner. It would normally seem a little much to have both items of furniture in one room, but the study was so large that Godwyn could be forgiven for keeping them. A single tall bookcase contained many work files, and Hesta looked forward to a time when she could to see if they contained any information she needed.

"This house is amazing. Are you going to keep it?" Evie asked.

Hesta picked up one of Godwyn's pens, the thick italic nib, speckled with dried ink, had not been cleaned for a while. She replaced the pen in the holder and glanced around the room. "I don't know. This could make a fine home, but it's a little big for me."

"It wasn't too big for Godwyn, though, was it?"

"No, you're right."

"You have time to think about it."

"What do I want with two houses?" Hesta asked.

"Seems to me, it gives you options," Evie said.

Even though Hesta liked the study so much she could see herself here all the time, one part of the room struck her as a little odd. There was a door in the corner. It looked like any other door in the house, except this one had two lock mechanisms and she possessed only one key.

"That door. It's bugging me. Godwyn was so well prepared, but I only have one key," Hesta said.

"Maybe it's hidden," Evie suggested.

"Yes, perhaps." Hesta opened one of the desk drawers and rifled through the contents. She repeated the process for all the drawers. She found no keys.

Evie looked in the escritoire, but she didn't find a key either. She did find lots of papers with strange markings on them, and she placed them on the desk for Hesta. "I know I haven't yet mastered the reading and writing thing, but this looks a little weird."

Hesta flattened the papers and laughed.

"What's funny?"

"I know what these are. I just need to put them in order."

"I don't see any numbers," Evie said.

"It's written in code. But a very simple one."

Evie frowned at her. "Well, that doesn't help me, now, does it?" she said. "Shall I go and get tea whilst you do the clever stuff?" She shuffled towards the door.

"Evie, stop!" Hesta said. "I'm sorry, that wasn't what I was trying to say."

Evie paused at the door and waited for Hesta to say something more.

"It's not a code, it's a language. This is how we wrote the silent speak."

Evie made an 'o' with her mouth, but no sound came out.

"Come look. Let me show you."

Evie didn't move.

"Please."

Evie crossed the room to stand next to Hesta. "All right, show me then."

"Silent speak is all about gestures of the face and hands, right? So long lines are a finger, and short ones are a part of one."

"And the thumb?"

"Is the angled line," Hesta answered. "The angle of the lines and how they are combined is important for words and single letters or numbers. Sometimes there is movement, so the curves there show how much and in what direction." Hesta pointed at the top left corner of every sheet. "Numbers are easy to work out." She counted with her fingers. "One line, two lines, etc., like the tally system. So he's written them as the silent speak words for one, two, three. Four and five are missing, but I have six."

"So what does it say?"

"Sorry. Needs must. Find a book," Hesta said.

"Which one?"

"On the next sheet, he says left three down, a tube to see a dragon." Hesta laughed.

"What's funny?"

Hesta looked at the left pedestal of the desk and opened the third drawer. "I looked in the drawers, remember? And in that drawer, left three down, there are actually two tubes, I suppose." She pulled them out and placed them on the desk. "A kaleidoscope toy, which makes patterns, and a spotter's scope." Hesta stood up and went to the bookshelves. She pulled out a book. "To find the dragon, the constellation, you need to look at a star map." Inside the book, under the information for the constellation of the dragon, she found another sheet of paper. "Number four. Which is also number five."

"That's clever of him, and very smart of you," Evie said.

"Thank you."

Hesta read through the instructions and shook her head. She opened the right desk drawer and pulled out a tablet of writing paper. She flipped through every page but they were all blank. One page had been ripped out, leaving a small part of the page still attached to the pad. That should have made identifying the paper concerned easy, but they couldn't find it anywhere. "What the hell is that about? All of that for nothing?"

"That's not like him at all," Evie said. "Maybe he was afraid someone would find it."

Hesta drummed her fingers on the writing surface. One edge was loose. She lifted it up and slid out a small sheet of blotting paper. "Well, that's not it." She threw it back on the desk in frustration, but the blotter slipped off the desk and landed on the floor.

Evie picked it up. "There are symbols here."

Hesta looked. "No, they look random to me, and the ink is all blurred." She stared at them for a moment. "Wait." She pulled out a piece of paper and copied the rather vague marks. When she was done, she took it to the window and placed the paper against the glass, but the wrong way round.

"If we add a little creativity to what he's put, this is a series of numbers." She stared at the images and then used a pen to write down the three number codes. She sat back at the desk with the papers before her. The excitement in her chest grew as the code started to make sense.

"And?" Evie prompted.

"It's page, line, and symbol," she said. She jumped to her feet. "Give me a hand, please. We need to move that escritoire a little."

The desk was heavy, but they managed to drag it forward. Hesta searched the wall first. Nothing. Then she looked at the back of the desk. The wood was a little rougher, it needed a polish, and a small leather flap by the leg looked a little suspect. She pushed her finger inside and touched metal. She grinned as she grasped the key and held it in the air in victory. "Guess what we have here."

She tried the key in the second lock and it opened without further fuss. She opened the door to reveal a small closet. There were shelves with ledgers on them and a large wall safe.

"Safe key," she muttered.

"What?" Evie asked.

Hesta grabbed her handbag and rummaged through until she found the small package Godwyn had given her months before. "Just in case," as he had put it. The package contained the safe key.

"He put a lot of effort into this," Evie observed.

"Yes," Hesta agreed. She wondered if the contents of the safe would explain why. It was always wise to be careful, but this went way beyond that.

She took the safe key, inserted it into the door, and twisted the three tumblers to the code that had been included in her letters from Godwyn's testament. Finally, she turned the heavy handle and the safe door opened.

There was money. Hundreds of pounds in thick bundles of notes.

Evie looked over her shoulder. "How much is that?"

"A lot," Hesta answered.

"You're a lady of independent means, then."

"I have been for a long while."

"I know, but still, have you *seen* how much is here?"

Hesta chuckled. "It's the paperwork I want to see. That might answer a few questions so I know what to do with his business."

"You do the papers, and I'll count the money," Evie said. "Not that I can count much, but I can move the notes from one hand to the other, if you like."

Hesta looked at the thick wad of papers in her hand. "I think this is going to take a while."

"How long? Are we going to look for this beast thing tonight?"

"Yes. I'll do what I can, and we'll go out after sunset, I think."

"That sounds good."

"Before we start poking around in here, don't you need to purge after sorting out Finn this morning?"

Evie looked sheepish and turned away. "I can't. I tried."

"We have to do something about that."

"I can't. Not right now. I don't know what to do."

"We'll figure something out."

"I hope so." Then Evie straightened her shoulders. "You better start looking at that paperwork. I'll put the money in piles of ten, and you can read."

"Okay," Hesta agreed.

She picked up a sheet of paper and pretended to read as she watched Evie over the top of the paper as she counted out piles of notes, checked them, and bundled ten of those short stacks into a pile. She found paperclips in the escritoire and secured the pile.

Hesta smiled to herself, it seemed that Evie knew more than she let on. What a life she had led. Hesta already knew that Evie had suffered, but sometimes it was the little things, like the fact that Evie felt she had to hide the things she knew, that got to Hesta. Her heart melted anew, and she resolved once more to ensure that Evie would never be placed in such a precarious position ever again.

Her mind set, she turned her attention back to the papers and began her task. She skimmed each sheet and placed them in one of a number of piles. One pile she mentally entitled 'operations.' These were notes about Godwyn's, and now her, properties and assorted business interests. She placed political papers to one side. There were not many of them, but they were instructive of his political opinions.

There were several sheets of paper that Hesta put in a

heap. She called this pile 'the slave trade.' She would match them with Godwyn's other businesses at some point to ensure they were no longer running. One sheet caught her attention.

"I think you want to see this," Hesta said.

"Sure," Evie replied, but she finished counting out the money in her hand first and clipped them together. "You do know that the money in this safe makes you doubly rich, don't you?"

"How much is a lot?"

"Three thousand Anglish pounds so far," Evie answered.

Such a large sum made Hesta pause. Then she shook her head. "Forget it, that's not at all important."

"But—" Evie started.

"Seriously. It's just money. I know it's a great deal of the stuff, but this," she waved the note about, "is far more important."

Evie stopped her counting. "What is it?"

Hesta returned her attention to the sheet of paper and the many others like it. "This is important. It's your bill of sale."

"Tell me what it says."

Hesta flattened the document. "Evierja Chjestka, and in pen above it they've put Evie Chester, aged 5." She looked up.

Evie had scrunched her eyes closed. "Go on," she murmured.

"You are from the village of Krachka, on the northern end of Kurdansk, Principality of Kurdjuska, and you were offered for sale by Karolinya and Havrolt Chjestka, your parents."

A sob escaped Evie. "Why would they do that?"

"It has a 'reason for sale' section." She paused. "Great Mother of us all, they sold you because you have witch hair and devil eyes."

"What does that mean?"

"Blonde hair and blue eyes," she answered.

"Anything else?" Evie asked.

"The purchaser's stamp and sign is Nevin Fowlkes, for, and on behalf of, the Blenheim Consortium of Eastern Iberica. From there, you went to the mines of Eflund, Kurdjuska. There isn't much after that, other than another sales stamp eight years later for Brangham Mercantiles. It's smudged, but it looks like you were on one of the Iberican islands. I can't be sure, but it looks like Hevlata, or is that Sholata?"

Evie sat at the desk, her face a blank and impassive mask. "Right. I think I'll just carry on counting," she said, and turned away.

Hesta wondered if she should leave Evie to process this information. She had to have known what happened. Or did she? She glanced at Evie, her shoulders slumped, and knew she couldn't leave her alone.

"Evie," she said, as she moved to her side. When she touched Evie's shoulder, Evie looked at her with sadness in her eyes.

"I knew most of that already, but when you see it on paper, and it is read to you, then it becomes a painful reminder of who you are." She snorted. "Not that it is easy to forget when you have an accent like mine."

"You were taken—"

"Not taken, Hesta. I was sold."

"You were only five when you were sold. I wonder why you didn't lose your accent."

"I spent eight years in a Kurdjuska mine. You stick with those who speak your language. By the time I went to the islands, I had spent most of my time with lifelong Kurdjuskan miners. They are not known for their gentle manners."

"I suppose not, but I think your accent is wonderful."

"Do you?"

Hesta lifted Evie's chin so she could look into her eyes. "This reminder of who you are tells me that Evierja Chjestka, or Evie Chester as she is now called, is an amazing woman who will prevail no matter what hardships are heaped upon her. It is a reminder that she, that *you*, are intelligent and thoughtful, with a big heart despite the fact that so many people have wished you harm. Your soul, Evie Chester, is as big as the world upon which we stand. I am reminded of these things not because of a document, but in spite of it."

For a moment, they looked at each other, and then Evie stood and threw her arms around Hesta in a tight hug.

19

Hesta didn't sit back in her chair until Evie let her go. "Are you all right?"

Evie sniffed and used a small linen handkerchief to wipe her eyes and her face. "I've always known what my life has been like, but to see it written down like this brings back memories I'd rather not have faced. And to have you learn everything…"

"I can never know the pain you've been through, nor what you feel now," Hesta said. "But I'm here if you need me."

Evie nodded. "I'll be fine. I'm always fine. But tell me—in the middle of all those papers, does it say how many slaves Godwyn bought?"

Hesta picked up a small sheaf of documents. "I don't know how many exactly, but I have two dozen slave chits here. From the looks of things, I think Godwyn always kept meticulous records. If he has only two dozen chits, then that is probably all he had."

"He might have lost one, or he may not have had proof of ownership if he bought them—bought us—from pirates and slavers," Evie said.

"I get that, except for one thing. See? When Godwyn had

no official chit, he wrote one out himself. More than half of these documents have been written by Godwyn."

"Oh!" Evie said.

"And another thing. There is a comment on almost all of them. Here, at the bottom."

"What does it say?"

"Sold. Released. Free," Hesta said.

"Can we find out and make sure they are, really, free?"

Hesta nodded. "Of course. We'll take all of this to Bethwood House, and tracking down these names will become a part of our function. We will find them and free any that haven't already been freed. That way we can check on each one of them."

Evie looked up. "Thank you."

"It's the least a Bethwood can do."

"Even so, I appreciate your effort," Evie said.

Hesta grinned, but didn't say anything more.

"After all that, I could do with a cuppa," Evie said.

"Me too, and I'm starving. I thought you were going to buy me luncheon?"

Evie laughed. "We've been busy. I'll see what there is here."

"Well, rush. If I don't get something soon, I'll eat the leather off this desk."

Evie chuckled as she left the study, and the sadness that had filled the room after looking at the slave chits vanished.

Alone, Hesta finished sorting the paperwork. Too much remained to be done, but she'd had enough for one day. It had waited this long; it could wait a little longer. She rose to her feet and stretched. Her lower back cracked as she moved the joints in her spine.

She grabbed the papers and took them back into the storage closet. When she opened the safe to put the papers inside, a stack of money, mixed notes of one and five Anglish pounds, spilled across the bottom. She straightened them up, but as she did so, the liner along the base of the safe moved. She lifted the layer of leather and found a small package pressed against the back wall. The paper, waxed against the damp, tied with ribbon and sealed with melted wax, bore a seal in black. For a moment, she stared at the package. Goose pimples rose on her arms and a cold shiver ran down her spine.

"Don't be silly," she said. Even then, it took another moment or two before she could stir herself to reach for the packet. She shuddered as her fingers brushed against it. The waxy paper felt greasy and unpleasant to her touch. She gripped it with her fingertips and rushed it to the desk. Relieved when she could put it down, she examined her find a little more closely.

The seal was not one she recognised. No one sealed anything these days, least of all in waxed paper and ribbon, but at least she knew it had not been opened. The waxed paper cover, a dirty off-white, made the contents difficult to see, but she could make out papers inside. Folded papers.

The door opened, and Evie came back in. She looked pleased with herself.

"What's given you such a cheeky grin?" Hesta asked.

"Tea is on its way, but I'll tell you now, Mrs Hobart makes the finest port pie in all of the Angles."

Hesta laughed, and the tension that had gathered at the back of her neck and shoulders lifted.

"You can have some as well when it arrives. And she has these sweet pickles I've never had before. We have to take some home with us."

"You've spent your time tasting all the food in the kitchen?"

"Haven't I just." Evie smiled shyly. "Can we come back again and try some more?"

"Don't you like Mrs Dunn's cooking? Or Agatha's?"

"Course I do, but really, you wait. You'll see. And then

you'll want to come back for more, too." Then she stopped in front of the desk. "What've you got there?"

Hesta gestured to the package. "I found it partly hidden at the bottom of the safe."

"I see. So you needed to find the secret key to open the locked door to find the safe, and then know to look for something hidden inside? Sounds suspect to me."

"Doesn't it just. I thought he wanted to hide the money, but now I find this. Who uses waxed paper and seals anyway?"

"Looks like one of those legal things to me. You know, when we see them legal men, they wrap things up like this."

Hesta leaned her elbows on the desk and rested her chin in the palms of her hands.

Evie pulled up a seat and sat opposite, the desk and package between them. "Are you going to open it?" Evie asked.

"I don't know if I should."

"Why not?"

Hesta sat back in her seat. "The truth is, it doesn't feel right at all."

"It's yours now, Hesta. You may as well look inside so you know what you have to do with it."

"I know."

They fell silent and stared at the package. A knock at the door interrupted Hesta's deliberations.

"Come in," she called out.

Mrs Hobart opened the door and Mr Hobart carried in a large tray, which he brought to the main desk. "Here, Miss Bethwood?" he asked.

"Yes, that's fine, thank you." She smiled at the contents of the tray. "That's quite a spread, Mrs Hobart."

"It's nice to get a chance to do what I do," Mrs Hobart replied.

"Please enjoy," Mr Hobart said, and ushered his wife out

of the room. "Let me know if there is anything you need. Just use the pull at the side of the fireplace, and I'll be here in a moment."

"Thank you, Mr Hobart."

He bowed and closed the door behind him.

Evie removed the cosy from the teapot and poured into two fine porcelain cups. She added a drop of milk to each and passed a cup to Hesta. "Now remember, the food here is incredible." She picked up a small dish filled with a dark pickle relish. "And this is wonderful." She grabbed a couple of cheese triangle sandwiches and added a good spoonful of relish to each one.

Hesta helped herself to a small slice of the much-vaunted pork pie. Although she'd been hungry, she couldn't muster the enthusiasm that Evie had for her food.

"You might as well open the package if you can't focus on your meal," Evie said.

"You're right." She grabbed Godwyn's letter knife and sliced across the ribbons under the seal. She broke the other seals and a flash of red caught her eye. "Did you see that?" she asked.

Evie sat with a pie-laden fork halfway between her plate and her mouth. "I saw."

"I'm not imagining it?"

"No."

"A flash of red?"

Evie put her food back on the plate and leaned across the desk. She seemed more focused.

"And?" Hesta prompted.

"It looks not-right. I didn't notice that before."

Hesta used the knife to flip over the seal, and on the back of the wax she noticed a small glowing symbol. It burst with colour once and then faded away to nothing. "Whatever it was, it's gone now." She took a deep breath to settle herself and waited for her heartbeat to settle. She used the knife to open the package, touching it as little as possible.

Inside, there were several sheets of paper. Thick and heavy paper, with another wax seal to keep it closed. Except Hesta recognised this design. She'd seen the stamp in the drawer. It had been one of her brother's affectations.

"This one is Godwyn's seals," she said.

"Must mean it's okay, then," Evie said.

Hesta didn't answer. She broke the seal and opened the papers.

"What does it say?" Evie asked.

"Give me a chance to read it," Hesta said. "It's a contract."

"For what?"

Hesta threw the first sheet down onto the desktop when she had read it. She knew she needed to spend a little more time reading in detail, but she got the gist of it. The second sheet followed the first.

Evie moved, but Hesta didn't notice until she gripped Hesta's shoulder. "I'm here," she said.

Hesta read on. When done, she threw the third sheet down, then read and discarded the fourth. She read the last sheet more thoroughly and then gathered the whole pile and reread them.

No matter how closely she looked at the papers, she couldn't change the words they contained. The documents fell from her fingers, and how her heart didn't stop beating, she would never know.

Evie pulled the chair around and knelt in front of her. She wiped Hesta's cheek, and it was only then she realised she had started to cry.

"Talk to me, Hesta."

"It's Godwyn," Hesta said.

"What about him?"

Hesta stared into Evie's eyes. "He sold me."

"What?"

"He sold me," Hesta repeated.

"Who the hell to?"

"Funny you should mention hell," Hesta replied, but she didn't look happy, nor did she look as though she'd made some joke. "He sold me to a prince of Hell, and all the things I thought were true aren't."

She stood up and grabbed the wastepaper basket as the small amount of pork pie she'd eaten came back up. Evie offered her a napkin and wiped her face.

"Why are you so nice?" Hesta asked.

"Because I think this is all pretty dreadful. You need a moment to adjust, and you need someone to be here for you. That would be me."

The world Hesta had known fell apart and changed. Her tears came then, but it was Evie who caught her and held her.

20

E vie settled Hesta in to her room at Bethwood House. She set the lamps to dim. Sunset had arrived with great determination, and Evie didn't want to leave Hesta in the dark. She sat at the edge of Hesta's bed, and although she wanted to stay with her, there were other things to do.

"Will you be all right here?" Evie asked.

"Yes," Hesta replied.

"I won't be long."

"I know."

"Any words of advice, or any suggestions?"

"No."

Evie sighed. She grabbed Hesta's hand, but it was limp in her grasp, as though Hesta couldn't be bothered. That was a worry. "Will you talk to me about it?"

"Yes."

"Good, shall I stay and we'll talk, then?"

"No. Go."

A part of Evie wanted to stay, but she wondered if Hesta needed time to process. She had to respect that choice. Her revelation would have been a lot to take in. Hopefully, given a little time, Hesta would be able to share her feelings.

"Right. I'll be out making myself the target for the beast. I hope it can sense that I am a part of it now."

Hesta looked at her with dull eyes. Even her skin looked washed out.

"Be careful." She spoke as though the effort of producing words was a chore. Request made, she sank against her pillows and pulled the blankets up to her chin.

"I'll be as fast as I can," Evie said.

She walked out of the bedroom, and Hesta didn't seem to notice her leave. Downstairs, she made her way into the kitchen. "Innie. Glad you're here."

"What can I get you?"

"I'm going out with Charlie in a minute."

"I know, love."

Evie tried not to smile at the term of familiarity. "We'll be fine, but Hesta, Miss Bethwood, is not at all well. And I don't think she's eaten much."

"I'll make her some broth. She'll feel better after that."

"I think it's best if she's not left alone for too long."

"Understood," Innie said. "I'll take care of her, don't you worry or fret."

"Good, that takes a weight off my mind." Evie grabbed her coat and dropped a fistful of coppers into her pocket, just in case.

Outside, she found Charlie taking care of the calash, making it ready for their evening ride. The lamps were lit and they ready to go.

"Do you know where we're going?" she asked.

"Yes, ma'am."

"Just call me Evie."

"Yes, ma'am." He winked. "Evie, then."

"Do you have a route?"

"Yes, ma…Evie. The quiet roads in and around the back of Ardmore."

"Good. Can I ride up front with you?"

"Sure, but it'll be cold."

"I'm fine. I might see more from there, and besides, this is all about making sure I'm seen."

"Seen?" he queried.

"Well, smelt really. I'm the bait."

"I hope we're not going to be in any trouble with just the two of us."

"We'll be fine, Charlie. " She hoped so anyway. "We just need to drive around a bit. This way we can chat, and I don't have to yell instructions."

"Yes, Evie. Shall we make a start?"

They drove a circuitous route through Salverton and in and around Cainstown. In spite of Evie's claim that they might chat, she couldn't think of anything to say. Her thoughts split between worry for Hesta and fear of the beast.

Halfway through Cainstown, a beggar boy flagged them down.

"Here, you! Get off with you!" Charlie yelled at the lad.

"Miss Chester!" the lad yelled.

"Pull over, Charlie, it's all right."

The boy didn't look more than ten years old, but Evie knew that on the street most kids never looked their proper age. Either too young from bad food, or tough and old before their years. Like slaves were.

She jumped down to the street so they could talk without shouting. "Yes? I'm Miss Chester."

"I know. Them blue eyes, miss, and the light hair sets you out. Anyway, I bin waitin' 'ere fer awhile."

"I'm here now."

"I got a message from Finn."

She dug into her pocket and pulled out a copper. She flipped the coin to the lad. "What did he say?"

"Finn's bin to tha Old Mother, and she says, 'Take care of 'esta, like. She must not be left alone.'" His voice changed as he quoted the words. He spoke very slowly and with great deliberation as though to ensure he didn't miss anything.

"Why?"

"I bin tol' no more."

"All right, ta. I have the message. Has anything been said about the beast?"

He shook his head.

"My thanks to you and Finn," she said, and clambered back into the wagon.

Charlie looked at her.

"We have a deal with the beggar boys. They give us news."

"And you sort out their problems?"

"Well, we'll try."

"Where to? Back home or carry on?"

"Carry on, Charlie. Innie is looking after Hesta. I have to do this."

As they drove through Ardmore, she kept her thoughts to herself. She had a great deal to think about as they clattered through the quiet main roads. On the side streets, there were even fewer people, and when she saw anyone, they were in groups, and most often, those groups were loud and drunk near one of the many public houses or gin palaces.

Off the side streets, there were even fewer people about, and when they reached the back alleys, they saw no one. The people of Ardmore had already found somewhere safer to be.

For a while, they sat along one of the darkened alleyways. She listened to the city at night.

"It's so quiet. Gives me the shivers," Charlie said.

"Me too, Charlie," she said, although most of her thoughts were with Hesta. "I'm not sure we can achieve much here, but maybe drive some more and make sure we can be seen."

"Do we have to be in Ardmore? It's so quiet here. Maybe we need to be where there are more people to entice the shadows of the city."

Evie turned and stared at Charlie. "Good point. We could go to Badesville, then Blest Hill, followed by a final look through Ardmore before we return to Bethwood House."

"Right you are, miss."

"Evie," she corrected him.

They were crossing the main canal line as it passed through Badesville when Evie had the first inkling that they were being watched. "Stop," she said. The hair on her arms stood on end, but she didn't say anything out loud; the last thing she needed was a spooked driver.

They were on top on the canal bridge when Charlie slowed to a halt. Even the horse grew still. Evie glanced along the still, dark waters of the canal, but saw nothing untoward. Behind them, the mostly urban spread of Badesville sat mostly in the dark. Some of the streetlights had been lit, but many of them remained dark.

Before them, and towering above the east end of the city, the embarkation and tethering towers of the Badesville Air and Cargo field spread out in bright and well-lit glory. Two airships were tethered at the southern towers, and lights illuminated their long silvery balloons. On the ground, the security lamps swept over the field with the regularity of a well-ordered clock.

Then the prickling at the back of her head vanished.

"Everything all right?" Charlie asked.

"Yeah, let's carry on, shall we?"

From there, they went through Blest Hill, and like Badesville, much of the area remained in darkness. Back in Ardmore, they stopped in one of the side streets, and Evie closed her eyes. Yet no matter how much she focused herself, she couldn't find that feeling of being watched again.

It was close to midnight when they reached Cainstown. They drove along roads illuminated by streetlights, and on side streets the shadows dominated but none of them moved. There were more people out on the streets here, even at this late hour, but they travelled in groups, never alone. When Evie and Charlie passed these groups, they stared at the carriage with suspicion. She didn't blame them.

Charlie drove them to the river. Now the lamps of Stake Island illuminated the water of the Vyon and cast sickly shadows over the distant banks. Evie shivered at the sight of the place—not from a feeling of being watched, but with the memory of her visit to the condemned men there.

"Are you all right, miss?" Charlie asked.

"Bad memories, that's all," Evie said. "Let's go home, Charlie."

"Right you are," he said.

He turned the carriage in the direction of Salverton, and Evie knew they were being watched again. Her skin itched, and when she looked at where she scratched, her hands glittered with darkness. They didn't stop glistening even when she reached Bethwood House.

Charlie said nothing. She hoped he hadn't seen the sheen on her skin.

Inside the house, Innie Dunn made them a warming cup of tea, but if there was anything odd about Evie's appearance, she didn't comment on it.

"Is Hesta all right?" Evie asked.

"Asleep, poor love," Innie answered.

"I'll see how she is when I go up."

"If she wakes, I think a sweet tea would do her good. There's nothing better than sweet tea."

"I agree. It's all right now, I'll see she is safe all night. You and Charlie should retire. It's been a long day."

"Don't you worry about anything else. I'll lock up," Charlie said.

Evie placed two cups of tea on a small tray and nodded. "Thank you."

21

At the top of the stairs, Evie opened the door, and soft yellow lamplight spilled out from Hesta's room. She crept inside and made her way as quietly as she could to the table. If Hesta was asleep, she didn't want to disturb her. The sleep would do her more good.

Evie placed the tray on the table and when she turned around, Hesta's eyes glittered. She was awake.

"It's late," Hesta said.

"I know." Evie picked up the cup of sweetened tea and brought it to her. "Sweet tea for you. Do you need help sitting up?"

"I'm not an invalid," Hesta said.

"I didn't say you were." She dragged the chair that stood next to Hesta's dressing table and placed it by the bed. "You should drink the tea."

"Why?"

"Because it will make you feel better."

"Why did you go out and risk yourself?" Hesta asked.

"We talked about this."

"But you went without me."

"Yes, I know. I'm the bait remember?"

"I remember what we talked about, but I'd still rather you didn't."

"I know that too," Evie said.

"Did anything happen?"

Evie wanted to say no, but that wouldn't help anyone in the long term. Besides, if she had been scented, the danger would come regardless. "I think I was observed," she said.

"By the beast?"

"Perhaps."

Hesta frowned. "I told you not to go. Now you've put yourself at risk."

Evie looked into Hesta's face. She was washed out and the dark circles under her eyes made them look almost black. Around her neck, her old scars glistened with those inner lights again. Evie had cured the curse, but there remained more to take away. She would have done so weeks ago, but Hesta always seemed reluctant to let her.

"Your scars are brightening again. I think it is because you're not well. Shall I take some more away?"

"No!"

Evie stiffened. "I'm sorry. I didn't mean to offend you."

Hesta looked away. "You'll make me feel things, and I'm not worth that. You don't want that."

Evie reached out until the tips of her fingers touched the side of Hesta's face. At first, Hesta resisted. When she turned to look back at Evie, there were tears in her eyes.

"Will you tell me what's wrong?" Evie asked.

"I can't," Hesta whispered.

"Is it because Godwyn, the brother you trusted, had you enslaved?"

A tear trickled over Hesta's cheek. "There's so much more."

"Tell me."

Hesta shook her head.

"All right." Evie reached for Hesta's tea. "You should

drink this, and then get some sleep. It's late. You need to rest." She smiled to put Hesta at her ease, but she wasn't sure if it worked or not. She rose to her feet. "I also need to rest. It's been a long day."

Hesta's eyes grew wide. "You're going to leave me?" She reached out, but Evie stood too far away to be touched.

"Just to get my things. To change." She pointed to the armchair in the corner of the room. "I'll sleep there and make sure you are safe all night."

"Don't leave me."

"I'll only be down the corridor. I'll come back."

"No. Please. Don't go."

"I need to get my night—"

"I have spares in the drawers," Hesta interrupted. "Just don't go."

Evie changed into one of Hesta's nightshirts and doused all but one of the lamps. She used Hesta's washstand to prepare for sleep and readied the armchair.

"Not there," Hesta said.

"Where then?"

Hesta shuffled to the side of the bed and pulled back the blankets and sheets. "Here."

"I haven't purged. It might not be a good—"

"Here," she repeated, but more firmly.

Evie thought about it for only a moment. A chair or a comfortable bed? The bed won. She slid into the bed and pulled up the sheets. It was warm and cosy next to Hesta. "Lights out?"

Hesta reached over to the lamp and doused the light.

"Good night," Evie said, and wriggled about to get settled.

Hesta moved to her side. "Hold me?" she whispered.

"If you want?"

"Yes."

Evie turned on her side and slid her arms around Hesta. It

was nice to be close to another person. No matter what, she would be there. She stroked Hesta's back to be as reassuring as she could. "It'll be all right."

Hesta sniffed. "Will it?"

Evie hugged her tight. "Of course it will. Now shush. Sleep. It will better in the morning."

"No, Evie, it will never be all right."

Evie wasn't at all sure how to make things better. "It will."

Hesta pushed away, and even in the darkness her eyes glittered. "How can it? I'm not even human."

"Is that important?"

"What? Of course it is. I'm not human, and I was sold to make someone rich and powerful."

"That's the past."

"Is it? Someone has to die soon."

"What? People die all the time," Evie said.

"No. Well, yes, but this time it was supposed to be me. How can I qualify if I'm not human enough?"

"You're human enough for me," Evie replied.

Hesta slumped against her. "Am I?"

"Yes, and tomorrow you can tell me everything. From what you are, to what you know. Of course, it would be even better if you were some beast yourself. Then when the howling creature catches my scent and comes a-running to rip me apart, you could jump in the way and scare the hell out it for me."

"Oh."

"Problem solved. Now can we sleep?"

Hesta snuggled up, her head under Evie's chin. She draped her arm around her waist and sniffed. "Yes, let's sleep."

Even so, it took Hesta a long time to fall asleep, and Evie listened to every breath she took until she did. Only then did Evie allow herself to join her in dreams.

E vie woke up in pretty much the same position she had fallen asleep. Hesta, her long dark hair cascading over pale sheets and pillow, was still draped over Evie's chest. For the first time, she truly thought she belonged someplace other than a slave pen. More, that she deserved more from life, too. A nice place to live, food, clothing, and someone to hold her.

She brushed Hesta's hair away from the side of her face and kissed her forehead. She no longer looked so pale or drawn, and in sleep she looked relaxed.

Hesta stretched in her arms, her eyes still closed. She murmured something incoherent and then sighed. "Evie," she mumbled.

"Yes?"

"Please tell me it was all a bad dream."

"Does this feel like a bad dream?"

Hesta nuzzled up against Evie so her breath brushed against the side of her neck. "No, this is a very nice dream." Her hand stroked Evie's side. "Nice dream," she repeated. "I'm not waking up from this."

Evie chuckled. "You aren't asleep, so you might as well open your eyes."

"If I do that, you might disappear."

"I won't."

"Promise?"

"I promise."

Hesta scrunched her eyes together even more firmly. "I'm not sure I dare believe you."

Evie laughed. "You can't get rid of me that easily, Miss Bethwood."

Hesta stiffened, and her eyes opened wide. "I'm not a Bethwood."

"See, your eyes are open, and I'm still here."

Hesta relaxed, but remained wary. Her gaze flitted from

side to side, as though she expected to find something, or someone, in the corners of the room. "Who am I?"

Evie brushed the back of her fingers against Hesta's cheek. "You are who you always were, and who you always will be."

"Who?"

"Yourself. You are the sum of all that you have done and all that you will do. Your decisions, your experiences, and all of your soul. Above all, you are who you decide to be." Evie lifted Hesta's chin and kissed her very lightly. "And to me, you are just fine the way you are."

"But everything is a lie!"

"Look at me, Hesta." She waited, then, for Hesta to focus on her face. "Am I a lie?"

She stared into Evie's eyes for a moment longer before she spoke. "No."

"If I am no lie, maybe other things aren't. Perhaps we need to look at this more closely."

Hesta slumped into the bedding. "Will it help?"

"Of course. But no matter what we find, it will all work out. Trust me."

Hesta stared up at the ceiling. "Remember when I told you that I thought I'd been cursed because I'd helped those women against the demon?"

"Yes, I remember that."

"I don't think it's true. Then, I thought it was because I had offended the daughter of some Prince of Hell, and I had. But that wasn't why I was marked." She held her fingers to her throat and drew her hand over the scarred and ravaged skin.

"I can make it better you know."

"Do you know what this is?" Hesta asked.

"Your curse."

"No, it's my slave mark." She turned on her side so they faced each other.

"Was that in the contract?"

"Yes. I was sold to Sasaan Isk, for favours." Hesta choked back a sob. "I thought we had escaped the rather dire circumstances of our childhood through hard work and my voice. Turns out that the riches and powers we have are because Godwyn bought them. With me as the price."

"I'm sorry, Hesta, truly I am. But you do have an amazing voice. I cannot believe your natural abilities didn't contribute."

The side of Hesta's mouth quirked upward in an almost smile. "There are lots of conditions. One of them is that I have to go to hell to repay Godwyn's debt."

"When is that?"

"On my thirtieth birthday," Hesta replied.

"Then don't have any more birthdays."

Hesta laughed. "I wish. Anyway, I could repay them at an earlier time if I chose to go. Or if they persuaded me to do so."

"Isk's daughter tried to take you, didn't she?"

Hesta nodded. "If the debt is not repaid and I find a way to thwart the deal, then I'll die and spend eternity in hell serving my owner."

For a moment, Evie wanted to take Godwyn's soul, if he even had one, and throw it at all the princes of Hell.

"One more thing."

"Go on, it'll be all right," Evie urged.

"I'm a half-demon abomination—a mixed breed—and I'm forbidden from contacting any of my family."

"Do you know who they are?"

"I haven't a clue."

"Then nothing to worry about yet," Evie said. She smiled. "We'll fix this."

"How?"

"Maybe we need to renegotiate the terms of your agreement."

"What?"

"I think we need to have a word or two with that prince of yours."

"He's not my prince."

"No matter. But it'll have to wait, because we have other things to think about right now. Like a certain beast that I suspect is coming for me."

"Evie, aren't you at all worried that you are lying in a bed with a demon?"

"No. Are you?"

"You're not a demon."

"We don't know what I am, so let's not get too bothered with what we think we know. Deal?"

"Deal."

22

O f all the rooms in Bethwood House, the library had become Hesta's favourite place. The journals of the gifted offered so many stories, lives she could clearly imagine thanks to the strength of the words inside each book. Sad tales, uplifting journeys of discovery and acceptance, and of course, tales of pain and rejection. Every journal, every person, had a life that needed to be saved.

She looked up from the book she had in her hand. Evie, in a chair by the window, was copying out words and letters, as she often did.

"How much longer before you can return to your duties at the hospital?" Hesta asked.

"Are you trying to get rid of me?"

"Not at all. Do you want to go back?"

Evie placed her chalkboard on the table and wiped the white dust from her hands. "Training to be a nurse is not foremost on my mind right now. I do want to be trained, it's important to me, it's just that I can't be myself, and matron…" Evie laughed. "Matron is someone who likes to be matron."

"She likes to be the boss of the young women in her control?"

"Oh yes, and throwing her position around suits her well. Anyway, although I need to learn more, it's not something I must do with any sense of urgency. That said, I do think we should go and see Doctor Montgomery tonight before we go out."

"Do you think so, being as you are under quarantine?"

"I'm not sick, Hesta Bethwood, as you very well know."

Hesta chuckled to herself. "I know. But no one believes you."

"There's nothing I can do about that. Are we still going out later?"

"Yes, Charlie will be ready for us a half hour or so after sunset. But I wish you would reconsider and stay here, safe at home. I'd be much happier if you did not put yourself at risk."

"I'm your best bet for bait, Hesta. If this infection calls to itself, then I have to assume whatever is in me will call out to the original source of the infection." She held up her hand. "I can't see it right now, but I know it's there."

"Is it really an infection?"

"No, but if we call it that, then it is just a sickness to those who don't understand."

"True enough."

"What if I ask you to stay home and safe?" Evie asked.

"The answer is no. If you go, I go."

"Fair enough, but I'm worried. What if I can't protect you. Or if we're infected, I can't heal you."

"Stop worrying. When we meet this thing, someone has to die," Hesta said.

"I know. That *thing* will die. Not one of us."

"But—"

"We'll figure it out," Evie interrupted. She almost sounded confident about it, too.

"Perhaps we will, but I would prefer to have more info—" This time the interruption came from a knock at the door.

"Enter," Hesta called out.

Charlie opened the door and walked in. "Evening, miss," he said. "The calash is ready when you are, but there may be a problem out on the streets."

"What sort of problem?" Hesta asked.

"The constabulary is everywhere, ma'am."

"Did you discover why they were out?"

Charlie nodded. "The constabulary has organised a city-wide beast hunt."

"Why would they do that?" Evie asked.

"Well now, someone, or something, chopped up a whole family last night in their home."

"Oh, that's dreadful," Hesta said.

"In Salverton, too," Charlie added.

Evie snorted. "I see. It's all right for everyone else to get slaughtered, but perish the thought that the more respectable sort in Salverton are under attack."

"Evie!" Hesta admonished.

"It's true, though, isn't it?"

"Yes, Evie, it's true," Hesta answered, and turned back to Charlie. "Will we be able to get through?"

"Maybe," he answered.

"Can we get to the hospital?" Evie asked.

"I would think so," he said. "They've got men and dogs throughout Queens Park already. After that, they'll clear through Salverton and the University District."

"The rich and powerful are taken care of first, of course," Evie said.

"And the distinguished areas of the well-to-do are easier to search. They have more space, fewer shadows, and fewer hidden places for some beast to hide," Hesta said.

Charlie nodded. "After that, they'll sweep through the rest of the city. I heard they've been calling for volunteers from the docks all day."

"In that case, let's give them time to clear this part of

town, and then we'll leave." Hesta looked at the clock on the edge of the desk. "Perhaps within the hour."

"Yes, miss. I'll be ready." Charlie inclined his head and left.

Hesta waited for the door to close behind him before she spoke. "Are you ready for this?"

"We had better be. I think this search will stir up matters rather quickly, and these people can't possibly deal with what they find."

"What *do* you think they'll find?" Hesta asked.

Evie lifted her shoulders. "A beast? A man? Whatever it is, the problem is nothing ordinary. Can we believe the words of one beggar boy?"

"About a huge furry beast that can jump impossibly high walls?"

"I think he saw something, but with curses and the like, who's to say what's real and what's part of the magic of the curse?"

"True enough."

"After we go to the hospital, we'll see if we can help out in the city."

"The constabulary won't like us getting involved," Hesta said.

Evie snorted. "I very much doubt that the constabulary will be able to maintain any control of the situation. Hopefully, the beast will come and find us before too many other people die."

"I hope so, Evie. I really do."

23

N o matter the time of day, the roads and byways through the residential areas of Salverton were rarely busy. On this particular night, they were more or less deserted. Whilst traffic through the streets had stopped, there were people about, Evie noted, but they were stationed inside the gates of several of the houses. Some, it seemed, took their personal safety seriously enough to hire men to protect them. She didn't blame them.

"Pull over, Charlie," Evie said.

Two men in thick black overcoats, carrying cudgels, stepped out of the shadows. Evie knew the type, she could recognize thugs for hire like Mr Grobber, streets away. No doubt they carried other concealed weapons.

"Move along," said one.

"Tell me what's going on," Evie called out.

"Trouble on the streets, miss. You should go home, like, and stay there until it's safe," he replied. At least this one was polite.

"I need to get to the hospital. How're things that way?"

"Should be all right, miss, but stay out of the way and get off the streets as soon as you can," he said. "Everyone carries a whistle, so if you hear them going off, head in the opposite direction. That would be the best thing."

"Right you are," Evie said. "Thanks for your time. Keep safe."

Evie didn't speak as Charlie drove them towards the hospital. She smiled to herself. Whistles. Of course, they had whistles. A constable's friend. Most nights a whistle or two could be heard, its shrill call through the darkness crying for attention. Instead of searching through random streets, they should have been listening to the whistles.

In front of the hospital, every light glowed bright, a beacon against the night sky. There were armed men around the perimeter here, too. Some carried rifles and shotguns, but they didn't interfere with the progress of the calash as it rolled towards the main entrance.

There, they saw a variety of nurses and medics, including Doctor Montgomery.

Hesta leaned closer to the driver's seat. "Charlie, pull up past the nurses. If they are waiting for a wagon, we don't want to be in the way."

As soon as they stopped, Evie opened the door and jumped to the ground.

"Evie, what are you doing here?" Joym asked. "You are still supposed to be in quarantine."

"I had half a mind to see about assisting you in the ward tonight," she said. "We also came for an update on the situation. We heard about the slaughtered family in Salverton but the details are a little sparce."

He nodded. "There are no updates as yet, but there maybe some soon. We're expecting more trouble."

"Trouble?" Hesta asked as she joined them.

"And you know what from," Evie said.

"I suspect," he whispered.

"Do the others have any idea what they are doing or what they will encounter?"

He looked away. "No. How could we raise the subject of, well, you know?"

"People will die if they are not properly warned," Hesta said.

"And not just the constables in the city, but the medics here and maybe the patients, as well. How could you leave them so unprepared?" Evie asked.

"We will do what we can and hope it won't be the same as the others," he said.

"Doctor, hope will do as much good as it has before. Hope does not counter a curse. You can't ignore this, and you can't make the bodies disappear into the fire."

"I know," he answered.

"You need to take a stand and admit that the gifted are useful at the very least. More than that, you need to encourage their help," Hesta said.

"It's not that easy," he said.

"Of course it's not easy," Hesta said. "But this is not going to go away just because it is inconvenient."

"Miss Chester," Joym said with added formality, "I understand this is an awkward moment, you should be at home, and yet you are here. Your skills would have a use I am sure."

"You mean my ability to deal with infections is beyond the skills of the mundane medic? Can you admit you need the services of a gifted one?"

"Please, Miss Chester, it is not appropriate to discuss this here."

"That is why you wanted me to look at the body in the Rotunda Hall rather than the morgue, isn't it? So no one knew you were consulting with the gifted?" Evie asked.

"I cannot be seen doing anything more than expected," he answered.

Evie looked at Hesta and then returned her attention to

the doctor. "Unless you accept that we gifted are an asset, I cannot help you. You'll have to manage as best you can."

"I agree with Miss Chester," Hesta said.

"For the moment?" he asked, his tone optimistic.

Evie shrugged. This was not a battle to be won so easily.

"While we're here, I have to wonder when Miss Chester will be permitted to restart her nursing duties," Hesta said.

"I would have to ask Matron Davids when it is safe. Two weeks is generally requi—"

"Except when she is needed," Hesta interrupted, "such as now."

"Maybe we could all get together and discuss a more equitable arrangement, for the subtle use of your skills," he suggested.

Evie snorted. "Let me know when it is convenient to be less subtle and actually heal people."

"Meanwhile, Miss Chester and I have a beast to catch before it fills your wards with dead." Hesta got back into her seat. "Take us to Ardmore, Charlie. We shall start there."

"Yes, Miss Bethwood," he said. He waited until Evie took her seat before he wheeled the carriage around and headed away. They left Joym on the hospital steps, but he didn't react to their departure.

Evie waited until the hospital was out of sight to ask, "What was that about?"

Hesta reached for Evie's hand and squeezed. "As he spoke, I had this horrible thought. I remembered how I found you after they'd tried to sanitize you. It sent shivers down my spine, and I felt so angry at them all. They didn't really care for you, did they? I know they have their systems and their ways, but Doctor Montgomery is familiar with our gifts, and he has made no allowances for you at all. The more I think about it, the madder I get. So mad, I could spit feathers."

Evie squeezed Hesta's hand in return. "How long have you been this angry?"

"Oh, I don't know. I think I've been irritated with them since the moment I found you in the shower room. Right now, though, I just can't seem to forgive them at all."

A cold fist closed around Evie's heart. Anger. Rage. These were not the emotions she associated with Hesta These were the emotions of the beast. Had Hesta been infected in some way? And why now? Fear and suspicion settled like stones in her gut, and she called up her gift and looked Hesta over.

"Evie, what are you staring at?"

Evie focused on Hesta. She appeared as she would normally appear, even the curse of her ravaged throat still glittered, albeit dimly.

"You should go home," Evie said.

"What? No!"

"This is not like you."

"How do you know what I—"

"Stop," Evie said. "Look at me."

Hesta turned in her seat so they faced each other.

'Can you hear me?' Evie tried to send to Hesta's mind.

Hesta frowned. "Yes, did you want to ask me something? We can't stay here all night."

"Can you not hear my thoughts?"

"No. What thoughts? I never pry into your thoughts, or even try that part of our gift until you ask," Hesta said.

"I tried to speak to your mind." She stared into Hesta's face for a moment. "There's something not right, and I don't know what it is."

"Don't ask me!"

"Why are you so angry?" Evie asked. "And why can't I talk to your mind?"

"Again, how should I know?"

"There you go again. Do I irritate you that much?" Evie asked. Hesta didn't appear to know how to answer, but Evie was prepared to wait until she figured it out.

"Maybe it wears out, like my kiss does?" Hesta asked.

"What, the anger?"

"No, the mind-speaking. Perhaps it's connected to my kiss. Maybe you can't speak to me, because my kiss no longer has the power to connect us."

"That's possible." Evie paused to consider the possibility. "That's given me an idea, if you're willing?"

"Sure. What do you propose?"

"A siren's kiss protects me from the song of a siren. What if I can impart upon you the magic of a syphon."

"Can you do that?"

"Yes? No? No idea."

"That's not very encouraging."

"Best I have right now." Evie leaned forward and pressed her lips against Hesta's. When she drew back, Hesta had her eyes closed. "How do you feel?"

Hesta slid her arms around Evie's shoulders and pulled her closer. "I think we need to try again."

"That's not what I—" she started to say. Her words were silenced by the next kiss. Yet this time, as they parted, she could see Hesta visibly relax.

'I feel better,' Hesta said into Evie's mind. *'Can you hear me now?'*

Evie grinned. *'I can, yes.'* She hadn't, until then, realised just how much their connection had meant to her. And now, everything felt right again. "What happened?"

"I've no idea," Hesta said. "I didn't even realise we couldn't *talk* anymore."

"I didn't, either. I thought you were just being polite and didn't want to force your thoughts on me."

"I wouldn't force any of my thoughts on you, and so I waited for you. I thought you just didn't want to be that close to me." She stared into Evie's eyes. "Or do you?"

Evie could hear the hopefulness in Hesta's voice. She spared a glance at Charlie, but he stared forward and attended to driving the calash rather than what they did or said. She turned her attention back to Hesta and smiled. "I think I do."

"I never wanted to impose my...mind speech on you." She smiled shyly. *'But it is nice to talk like this.'*

"This is so new to me, but yes, I feel more settled now."

"Good. Me, too."

Evie smiled and tried to hide the heat that rose in her cheeks.

"Now we're ready again," Hesta said.

"Yes," Evie agreed. "We are."

24

O nce across the river, the calash took them down the almost deserted main road through Salverton. They were stopped and then waved on as they joined Ardmore Street, which spanned the city from east to west. The road, bright with streetlamps, connected Salverton, Cainstown, and Ardmore to the main cargo terminus for the city's air freight.

Charlie drew the calash to a stop halfway through Cainstown and cursed loudly enough to be heard.

"What's wrong?" Hesta asked. She stood up in the carriage so she could lean out to the side and look forward.

Evie joined her, and when she leaned far enough, she spotted a dozen men across the street.

"Constables, as well," Hesta said. She sat down again. "Well, they'll be a little harder to pass."

"Perhaps," Evie said.

Two constables, with the backing of the men with them, stood to both sides of the calash. "Ladies," said one, "this is not the evening to be out on a pleasure drive."

"Why not, constable?" Hesta asked.

"Bit of a manhunt going on, ma'am. You should turn around and go home."

"I live on Ardmore Street, number seventeen," Evie said.

"Oh, yes?" He didn't sound convinced of the truth of her words.

"It's the guesthouse run by Agatha Hickman. Do you know it?"

"No," he answered.

"I do," one of the men behind him said.

"Is that right?" the constable pressed.

"And then we'll be on our way to my house. If there are any problems, you can send someone there. I live at Bethwood House in Salverton, if you need to check," Hesta said.

Although the street had several lamps lit, the constable raised the lantern in his hand and shone the light into the carriage. He looked confused for a moment. "Miss Bethwood?"

"Yes," she answered. "Or perhaps I remind you of someone else? Maybe you've heard of me as Hesta Estrallia."

"Pardon me. It's been a long time since your last performance, and I hardly recognised you," he said. "Sorry to hear about your brother."

"Thank you."

"It's not a good time to be out on the streets. You should go straight home. Do you need a constable to ride with you?"

"We'll be fine," Hesta said. "We'll head straight to the house."

"Right you are," he said.

"There are a lot of men on the streets. Do you know who you are looking for?"

He shook his head. "Not yet, but we'll be seeking him out every day until he's caught, don't you worry. When the dogs are ready, they'll bring them through Salverton down to Ardmore. Best be off the streets by then."

"We'll do our best," Hesta assured him.

He waved to the men around him. "Let them through."

"Drive on, Charlie."

"Are you taking me home?" Evie asked.

"No. Why would I do that?" Hesta asked.

"Because you told the constable we were going straight to the house."

"I did. But I didn't say anything about stopping there, did I?"

Evie chuckled. "Very true. I'll have to make sure I'm always very specific when I talk to you."

"Then we wait to see if we hear any whistles."

In Ardmore, Charlie pulled the calash over to the side of the road.

There were people on the streets, but fewer than Evie would have expected and they were all walking in groups. Even the public houses were open so far as she could see. Lights blazed out into the streets. With the smell of pipe smoke came the smell of beer and spirits.

"Where do you want me to wait?" he asked.

"Actually, if you drive on a little further, there's a side street by the gin palace. That would be a good place to stop," Evie said. She hoped the constables weren't blocking the side streets off yet.

"On my way," Charlie said.

At the gin palace, there were two other carriages parked along the side, the drivers hunched over as though they could merge unnoticed into the background. There were a few people outside, all drunk and using the sides of the building for support. That was normal.

From the gin palace, the sound of a piano, with the accompaniment of raucous singing, rolled outside whenever anyone opened the doors to let out the smoke and stink of gin and bring in some fresh air.

"We'll never hear anything here," Evie said.

"Perhaps, but no one will bother us either, will they," Hesta replied.

Evie sat back in the seat and grunted.

As they waited, the night grew still and cold. The gin palace emptied and long before midnight, the lights went out inside and the last remaining gin-sodden punters left the building.

"I don't think anything is going—" Hesta started to say. In the distance, a single whistle called for attention.

"That might be nothing," Evie said.

"And it might be something," Hesta replied. "We need to get closer. Charlie, head towards the whistleblower."

"I'm not sure where it's coming from," he said.

"Head down this road and bear left, I think," Evie said.

At the bottom of the street, they heard several other whistles joining the first.

"I think they're in Blest Hill," Charlie said.

"Get us closer, please," Hesta said.

"And fast," Evie added. She clutched her hand to her chest. Her heart had started to pound, but she wasn't sure whether it was with fear or anticipation.

Hesta shuffled forward to the edge of the seat, as though that would make the drive faster. At the southern end of Ardmore, the roads became little more than tracks, the ground wet and muddy enough that Charlie had to slow down. In the distance, the whistles grew louder and more frequent.

"I was mistaken. They're not in Blest Hill," Charlie said. He stopped the coach and stood up on the footboard.

"Charlie?" Hesta asked.

He cocked his head to the side. "Not Blest Hill. It sounds to me like it's close to the cargo terminal."

"Head straight there," Hesta said.

"I can't turn about in this lane, Miss Bethwood, so it might be best to carry on to Blest Hill, circle north before the terminus, and come back to Ardmore from the east, if that's all right with you?"

"Sounds good, Charlie," Evie said. "Do it."

They circled the edges of Blest Hill and raced along streets that were far too quiet for this time of night. They crossed the southern loop of the Vyon river and passed beyond the aromatic sewage and water works. Lights illuminated the works, but they were nothing in comparison with the brightness of the airship terminus. At least they could see well here. They raced around the edges of the loading areas and joined Ardmore Street at its very end. There were no houses here, this close to the air field, but ahead, after a slow sweeping bend, the outskirts of Ardmore began.

The whistles, however, had gone silent.

"Did we miss it all?" Evie asked.

"Charlie, just head along Ardmore until we see something," Hesta said.

Almost as soon as they'd cleared the bend and the first couple of houses, they saw a few people in the middle of the street. Evie recognised the uniform of a constable even at this distance.

Closer, she saw another group a little further along, but they stood a ways back from whatever had caught their attention.

"Nice and slow, Charlie," Hesta said. "Let's make sure we see all there is to see."

"Yes, ma'am."

A constable stepped in front of the carriage and called them to a halt. "Sorry, you don't want to go this way," he said.

"Why not?" Hesta asked.

He looked uncomfortable. "Someone has been hurt. We think it's by the same person who did all the others."

"The Butcher of Bristelle?" Hesta asked.

"Likely so, miss, yes," he replied.

"I should take a look, maybe I can help. I'm training to be a nurse," Evie said.

"I think it's a bit late for that, miss."

Evie whipped open the door to the carriage and stepped onto the road. "It would be a disservice not to do what I can, constable."

"No, miss, you better not approach. It's not for young ladies to—"

"Nonsense," she interrupted. "Everyone should get medical attention." She strode towards the group and realised what he meant. In the street, with surprisingly little blood to Evie's mind, lay a torso. At a glance, she could see no legs, arms, or head anywhere nearby.

"I see. Where's the rest of him?" she asked.

"No idea," the constable replied.

"Have you called for the wagon? There's no need for a medic or an ambulance," she said.

"Miss, this is not really for the fainthearted," he said, and tried to steer her away.

"No, I'm fine. I've seen far worse in the morgue," she said. "Although some argue when they are taken apart on the autopsy table, that is the worst time." She stopped half a foot away from the body and knelt down. She called her gift, and although she could see some evidence of the curse that she associated with the butcher, this one didn't possess that dark glittering life of an infected curse. This one would not be a problem. She prodded the body and even held her fingertips against the armless shoulder.

"Interesting," she said.

Behind her, someone started to retch. She rose to her feet and turned around. "Get the hell away from the body if you haven't the stomach for this." She glared at the poor chap until he made his way to the side of the road. He wouldn't be much use. She looked at the others. Most of them were a little green around the gills.

"You should tell them all, constable, not to interfere with the body if they have a weak stomach," she said harshly.

"Yes, miss," he answered.

NITA ROUND

Evie resumed her consideration of the torso, but there was nothing much to gain from her examination. Or was there, she wondered.

"His limbs have not been surgically removed," she said.

"How can you tell?" he asked.

"It would be a cleaner and more precise cut.". She knelt down and looked closer. "They are almost torn round the edges. But I'm not qualified enough to say with certainty what that means. A dull weapon, maybe? Something with a ragged edge? Or maybe even ripped off?"

He shuddered. "None of that sounds like a good thing."

"No, it isn't." She lifted the body. "Got a light?"

Someone, she didn't pay much attention to whom, shone a light under the torso. There were a few remnants of clothing, but they were soaked with blood. "As I thought. Freshly killed. Now, where's the rest of him?"

He pointed further along the street. "There's a leg."

"Then I need you to set someone to guard this body. Don't touch it. And you can escort me to the next part so I don't have to keep explaining myself."

"But, miss, I can't do that. I have my orders, and I'm already breaking them by letting you near."

"Don't fret. Just tell them all I've said and ask for Doctor Montgomery, the Dean of the University. He is experienced in this matter. Tell him to concentrate on the back of the neck."

"Yes, miss. But you shouldn't be here at all."

"I think you need all the help you can get, constable. Whoever did this is going to keep doing it. Even with everyone prepared and looking for trouble, this man has been murdered under our very noses. Do you think the Butcher will stop?"

"No, miss."

"Too right." She walked halfway back towards Hesta. "Coming? Charlie can follow on."

She waited for Hesta to join her. "This is going to get messy."

Hesta looked over her shoulder at the torso. "I can see that. This is a nasty business."

"Yes."

Hesta shivered.

"Will you be all right? It's going to get worse, I think, before it can get better. But if there is trouble ahead, we'd better stay together."

Hesta nodded. "I'll be fine."

"Sure?" Evie asked.

Hesta didn't answer.

25

E vie, with Hesta next to her, approached the next body part with greater thought and deliberation than she had the first one. She knew, at least in principle, what they would find, so she had little need to stare at the men in the road. Instead, her gaze took in the buildings around them. Darkness swallowed them all, and the streetlamps, even those lit, were less frequent than they were in the areas closer to the heart of the city.

From the corner of her eye, the shadows stretched and contracted. Evie shivered. She could not shake the feeling that they were being watched. The hair on the back of her neck stood on end. Hesta hooked her arm through Evie's, but she didn't slow down.

In front of them, a constable stood in the middle of the road, and two others stood off to one side. The constable planted his feet apart and swung his lantern so as to see them better, making the shadows shift even more. "Hey!"

Hesta stiffened at her side, but she didn't try to retreat. "Officer," Hesta said, and waved.

"Excuse me, ma'am, official business here. If that is your

carriage coming up, then you should get in and leave immediately."

"Of course it's official business. We've just looked at the remains along the way there," Hesta said. She gestured up the road.

"Constable Weyton permitted this?"

"He did, Constable…"

"Perkins," he answered.

Evie looked him over. He was not terribly old, and even in the weak light, he looked pale. "Well, Constable Perkins, my name is Evie Chester. I've been in training at the university, and I can tell you I've seen many a disturbing thing in the morgue, deep in the bowels of the hospital. Weyton seemed glad of any information we could offer."

"Did he now?"

"He did truly," Hesta replied.

"What part or parts did the butcher gift to you?" Evie asked.

He seemed to think for a moment and then gestured to a jacket on the ground. "A leg."

"Can I look?" Evie asked.

He shrugged. "If you need to."

"I do," Evie said, and she strode with great determination towards the coat-covered remains. She lifted the corner and exposed the leg. Some material, pale but almost soaked through with dried blood, clung to the knee. She knelt at the side of the limb but didn't touch. Yet. Little blood had seeped into the ground, but the wound remained red and raw. Her gift rose without the need to call for it, and in the leg, she saw the signs of the curse. More so than the torso. Much more.

"It's not from the same body," she said.

"Dear Mother of us all," whispered the constable. "Do you mean there are more bodies?"

"I do," Evie said. "Would you turn the leg over?"

"Oh, I ain't touching that thing," the constable said.

Evie looked at Hesta and took a step back. "I don't really want to touch this either," she said. "I fear I'll catch something."

"Don't," Hesta muttered quietly. "Don't touch it."

Evie took a deep breath. "I must." She reached out, and almost the moment her fingers touched the cool, dead skin, her gift burst into life and the infection raced into her with such force it took her breath away.

"Evie!" Hesta cried out.

She held up her hand to halt Hesta's rush. "It's fine." She stood up slowly. "Constable, have you a clean handkerchief? Or if not, then a piece of clean paper and a pencil?"

He handed Evie a sheet of paper from his small notebook and a pencil. She knelt beside the leg and jabbed the pencil into the wound. "I should get equipment for this kind of job," she muttered, more to herself than anyone else. She wiped the pencil tip onto the paper and nodded.

Hesta looked over Evie's arm. "What's that, a hair?"

"Yes, like the other at first glance. Joym will know more when he can look more closely." She folded the paper so the hair was wrapped safely inside and handed the small package to Perkins.

"When they come to take this away, hand this to Doctor Joym Montgomery and tell him this is the same killer. But this leg definitely means that there are at least two people dead. This one has been dead longer than the torso. Lividity is present here but not there. Got that?"

"Yes, ma'am," he replied.

"And the other body parts?"

"Keep on this road, you'll see Constable Allam. He will guide you. Best take your carriage, though, as it is a fair walk."

"Many thanks. Keep safe," Evie said.

"No one will be safe until he is caught," Perkins said.

When they got into the calash, Evie knew that Hesta was not happy.

"Did you have to do that?"

"Do what?"

"Touch the body. You absorbed more of that infection, didn't you?"

"I did."

"Why? You couldn't get rid of the first lot, now you have more. When will it make you sick?"

"Not yet. And probably not ever," Evie said.

"How do you know?"

"If it was going to make me sick, then it would have done so by now."

"You can't be certain." Hesta threw herself into her seat and folded her arms across her chest. "Why are you risking yourself in this way, Evie? Why?"

Evie turned sideways to face her. "We've talked about this."

"That was then."

"Did you see what that butcher left on the streets for people to find?"

"Of course I saw."

"He's baiting us. The constables have no chance against this killer."

"But Evie, it's not your job to put yourself at risk," Hesta said.

"I'm not sure I am at risk," she lied.

"Yes, you are. And you know it, too. You have that look in your eye and a most determined set to your shoulders. I think you know more than you let on."

Evie chewed at the inside of her cheek as she thought things through. "All right, then. I do think I know more, but I can't say much to these people. They would have me locked away."

"Why?"

"We are not looking for some madman with knives."

"It looks that way to me," Hesta said.

"It's not a 'he,' it's an it." Evie took a steadying breath. "Remember what the beggar lads said about Sparky?"

"I remember. He claimed he'd seen a beast of some kind, but no one seemed sure if he had or not."

Evie nodded. "Yes, well, the more I see, the more I'm inclined to believe him. Because the neck of that body looked chewed. I saw a bite mark in the skin."

"Are you sure?"

"As sure as I can be given the body bits I've seen."

Hesta winced at the thought of bits.

"And whatever this curse is, I carry it. And if it is a beast, it knows I have it."

"So you're absorbing more of the curse to make sure the butcher knows you're here."

Evie smiled to herself. "The beast already knows. I can feel its eyes on me. He's somewhere in the shadows. And if I don't understand him better, then we'll not be able to fight him well enough to win." She placed her hand on Hesta's arm. "I know this is scary—"

"Scary?" Hesta interrupted. "I'm terrified, and I worry because you don't seem to be at all concerned."

Evie stared at her hand against Hesta's skin and pulled it away. Nothing had happened, but she might have purged into her without thinking, and she hadn't even considered protecting Hesta. She needed to be more careful. "The sooner this is done, the better. A little bit more, and then we'll go home."

"Really?"

"We'll see," Evie said.

26

As they drew closer to the city center, the houses grew closer together, the streetlights grew more frequent, and the roadways grew brighter. In the distance, the baying of dogs warned of the incoming canine patrols, though Evie suspected they would cover north of the Vyon river first and work their way towards the body parts.

The carriage came to a staggered junction, with roads running north and south across Ardmore Street. Two constables stood on the southwest corner next to a small school. To the north stood two more constables who studiously avoided looking at something close to the wall of a house.

"Halt here, Charlie," Hesta said.

Evie was out first, and she strode along the road as though she had every right not only to be there, but to take control. "Constables Weyton and Perkins sent me. Which one of you is Constable Allam?"

A tall man with skin the colour of the desert Rabians stood forward. "I am he. Who are you?"

"I am Evie Chester, and I've been—"

"Under whose authority are you in the vicinity of this crime scene?" he interrupted.

Evie had no real authority so she avoided the question. "I've examined the other two attacks. If I could examine these as well, I might—"

"So you have no authority here."

Hesta joined Evie and placed her hand on Evie's shoulder. Her gift brushed against Evie's ears. "I am Hesta Bethwood, and—"

"I don't care if you're the King of all the Angles. You have no business here. Go home," he ordered.

"We have assisted Doctor Montgomery in the morgue on this particular case," Evie said.

"Bring the appropriate paperwork from the medics, and I'll give you access. Until then, the answer is no."

"But…" Evie started. The shrill call of a whistle and the yelp and whine of dogs interrupted her thoughts. She looked at Hesta. "Never mind, let's go."

Allam must have known what they were about. He followed them to the calash. "Please don't say you are heading off to the whistles?"

"That's our business," Hesta said. "You look after your scene, we'll look after ours. A pleasant evening to you." She banged on the door. "Ahead, Charlie, we need to be with the whistles."

"You're insane, the two of you. Take my advice and go home," Allam shouted to be heard as they drove away.

Evie waved at the constables as Charlie drove down Ardmore.

They travelled so far they almost reached the Hickman house at number seventeen.

"Do you want to see if they are safe?" Hesta asked.

Evie shook her head. "No. As long as they've stayed indoors, they should be all right. Besides, I think it's a bit late for a social call."

A howl pierced the night, and the calash swerved across the road. Charlie fought to keep the carriage upright, but on the seat, Hesta and Evie were thrown from one side to the other.

"What's that, Charlie?" Hesta asked.

"Ole Bess took fright. Something has her spooked," he said. As though to prove him right, their horse, Bess, pulled back so hard, she banged into the calash. She almost jumped into the air, but instead rose onto her hind quarters and tried to jump out of the way.

"Steady on, ole gal," Charlie soothed.

"Turn her around and go back a ways until she calms down," Hesta said.

"I don't know what's wrong with her," he said.

"Wrong? I think she has it right," Evie said. "I'll get out here. You'd better make sure she calms down. I think I'll take a look to see what has her so spooked."

"Me too," Hesta said.

Almost the moment they were out of the carriage, the calash spun about and clattered away with some speed.

"There goes our ride," Hesta said.

"She was terrified," Evie said.

"She's not the only one."

"You could—"

"No, I'm staying with you," Hesta interrupted. "We did say we'd best stick together, and now is not the time to bow to my fear."

Evie reached out and took her hand. "Then we will walk a little way to see what we can find."

"I don't hear any whistles."

Evie didn't reply. Silence filled the streets in a way strange to a city like Bristelle. The pubs had closed. Normal people were abed. Only the constables, the forces of the manhunt, and the beast walked the streets. She couldn't even hear the noises of the factories, which ran day and night.

Then the howl came again. Closer.

A whistle shrieked, and stopped suddenly.

Evie turned to Hesta. "It's close," she whispered.

Ahead of them, three men raced from a side street that headed to the river. If they went due north, they would reach the quays that the ferrymen used to get fares for river crossings. These men had no interest in ferries, she suspected. Three dogs followed the men, their leashes left attached and dragging across the ground behind them.

"Well," Evie muttered, "looks like we head towards that street.

"Markins Street," Hesta said.

"We'll head there, then."

Hesta gripped Evie's hand tighter, but Evie didn't complain. An ominous silence filled the street, and the clack of their heels sounded far too loud.

A shadow grew out of Markins Street, and they stopped walking. The shadow kept growing, until something big and silent stepped out of the darkness and turned to face them. Black and hairy, it stood on two legs and reached a little over six feet tall. Evie had expected something a little larger.

Glowing yellow eyes sat atop a large snout, and two shaggy, pointed ears flipped back and forth until it spotted them. Then the ears flipped forward. The creature raised its head and sniffed in their direction. It snarled and started to cross the road. Its big head shifted from side to side as it sniffed the air, and then it followed the men and the dogs into the street opposite.

Evie took a deep breath. Hesta's fingernails dug into her hand, but the pain felt reassuring. This was something normal. What she had seen was anything but.

"What the hell was that?" Hesta breathed.

"That, I think, is the beast. The Butcher of Bristelle is an animal after all."

"No animal walks on two legs, Evie. That's no normal creature."

Evie couldn't think of a response. The beast burst from the side street where it had disappeared, lowering itself onto all fours. It raised its head and sniffed the air.

Then turned its glowing eyes towards them and took a step.

"Well, bugger," Hesta said, as she took a step backwards.

The beast rose up on two legs again, and took another step in their direction. It opened its mouth and roared. Evie wasn't sure what was worse: the roar of the beast the huge mouth filled with teeth, the large muscular arms that ended in great, inches-long talons, or the fact that this huge beast was coming for them.

"Get behind me," Evie said. She stepped in front of Hesta and moved forward. That was where her bravery ended. Her heart pounded and her stomach churned so badly, she swore she was about to be sick.

No, she told herself, she would show no fear. Instead, she began to walk towards the beast as she called forth her gift.

The creature glittered with darkness. Not just a trace of the magical darkness as it had with the bodies. This beast was all curse, with an energy that had no place here in Bristelle, or any place else on this earth. It growled at her, and even from this distance, the stench of fetid breath staggered her. The smell reminded her of death and rotting meat. Of course this creature had killed far too many people to smell of anything but death.

Short fur that covered its legs and abdomen. Longer hair hung around its neck and chest down to the flat and sharply muscular belly. Further down, she could determine this was a he, not an it. Now that she thought about it, she wasn't surprised.

The beast expanded his chest to draw in a long rasping

draw of air. He roared, and rage washed over her in another wave of hot, fetid breath.

Hesta started to sing, and not with the subtle use of her gift that Evie had experienced before. Now, she sang a quiet lullaby, and as the siren's song reached Evie's ears, even she felt the need to sit down and relax. She shook off the tiredness. She needed to touch the beast and try to take it down.

Carefully, she walked towards it.

The beast growled at her and jumped forward. Evie moved to meet the creature. She was determined to kill it, even if she had to die to do so.

She raised her hands to touch it, and it swiped at her with such force she flew through the air and slammed into the short walls that surrounded the front yards of the houses opposite. Burning, searing pain ravaged her side. She touched her ribs. Her clothes had been shredded and dark liquid spilled to the ground. The blood, however, was nothing compared to the pain of breathing. Evie rolled onto her back and stared up at the streetlight.

Hesta's scream pierced the darkness, but she could do nothing about it. She stared into the light and even in the brightness, the darkness started to close in.

27

Paralyzed with shock, Hesta could do nothing as the creature struck at Evie. She managed a scream, but even that faded at the sickening thud of Evie striking the wall and slumping to the ground. She would never forget that sound. Evie, brave Evie, who could face this beast, lay on the ground, probably dead. Hesta knew she would be next.

The beast circled her as though looking to find the best place to bite her. It toyed with her, but she couldn't escape it. Stinking breath brushed across her face, and the smell of it took the strength from her legs. She couldn't fight this creature. How could she, when the only weapon she had was her song, which hadn't worked the first time.

Hesta turned her eyes heavenward. She only had one thought: *I'm going to die.*

"Forgive me, Great Mother of us all. Forgive me for all the wrongs I have committed. I'm ready to return to the divine spirit. Think well of me."

Gleaming teeth stopped a few inches in front of her face. The beast sniffed her, and then a long tongue rasped against her cheek.

She stood frozen, stuck without any way of defending

herself or injuring this creature, even if it was an overgrown dog...

The direction of her thoughts faded away. Dog. Yes, it was rather larger than a dog, being a cursed beast, but she wondered if seeing it that way would help.

Hesta swiped at its muzzle, and her fingernails grazed its nose. Its head recoiled, and a subtle yelp escaped its mouth.

"Go away, you stinky furbag. I can tell you now, if she's dead, I'll kill you."

The beast paused a moment and wiped its muzzle. His lips curled in a snarl, and he regarded her through bright, unnatural eyes.

She didn't have much time to wonder what his expression meant. He opened his jaws and roared.

With a degree of courage she didn't know she possessed, Hesta roared back. Too deep to be a scream, but she filled her voice not with a song, but a siren-powered cry of anguish. A screech like a hundred claws dragging across a chalk board.

The beast yelped and backed away until he was hunch over against the wall. His ears fell back almost to the point where they lay against his neck. He looked at her sideways, the whites of his eye showing.

She stopped screeching and rushed to Evie. If the beast was going to attack her, then let it. She needed to find out if Evie was all right. It was all she could think about.

As Hesta rushed toward her, Evie sat up and shook her head, as though to clear her thoughts. She rose unsteadily to her feet, clutching her side. Even with thirty feet between them, Hesta saw Evie's wince of pain. When Evie tried to speak, no words came out. '*Hesta*!' she silently cried. '*I'm not sure how long I can do this alone. I need your strength if we are to survive this.*'

'*I hear you,*' Hesta replied into Evie's mind.

'*You scared it?*'

'I screamed at it, but I don't think the effect will last long.' As she spoke to Evie, the creature stood up again.

Evie bent down and picked up a stone from the ground. "Beast," she said, and it came out as a whisper. Then she threw the stone at it. It was only thirty feet away, but even that close, she couldn't generate enough force to cause damage. The beast roared at her.

'I need you to touch me,' Evie said. *'I can't walk far right now.'*

Hesta closed her eyes for a second to steady her nerves as she approached Evie with slow and tentative steps. Even after her attempt at bravery in the face of those teeth, she couldn't maintain her courage. She lifted her voice in song, something that always made her feel better.

She sang of strength for Evie, and she put so much heart into her skill that her voice surged with power. Evie needed her and she would give her everything she had. Her strength grew and blossomed in every tone and every note, and poured, without contact, to where Evie stood.

Evie drew her shoulders back and stiffened. She grinned as she held her hands out at her sides. A purple glow lit her fingers, and bit by bit, crept up her arms, over her chest, and covered her with a subtle magenta glow. Even her hair brightened and glittered with the unnatural light.

'Will you need to touch it?' Hesta asked.

'Stand next to me,' Evie answered.

'What are you—' she started, but her thoughts were distracted as the beast roared once more and loped in their direction.

Hesta almost froze in place, but she needed to keep up the power of her song, for Evie as much as anything else.

The beast batted at his ears and roared. Even this song he did not like. He raised his paw to swipe towards Evie, but he stopped as a wave of dark light rushed from the him to her.

Evie's hands glowed and sparkled as wave after wave of darkness flew into her. She jolted at every point of contact, and to Hesta, she looked as though she was in great pain, but she didn't stop. If anything, Evie gritted her teeth and grew even more determined.

Hesta could not help but feel pride, not only for what she could do, but for her fortitude and resolve.

It was only then that she realised what they had achieved. Siren and syphon, joined by will not touch, and although separated by no more than a few feet, the power still flowed.

The beast could not fight them together. He seemed frozen in place, unable to react to either song or syphon. The creature sank to his knees. His snout receded and flattened. The short hair across his chest thinned, some retracted into his skin and the longer hair detached and fell to the ground. He folded in on himself and crouched on the ground. He whimpered as he shed more hair, until only pale skin remained. He had dark hair on his head and a mat of black hair on his chest. He howled, but with a voice all too human.

Now, he was just a man, and a pretty unexceptional specimen at that.

Evie fell to her knees. The purple glow vanished, and she glittered with a darkness that absorbed and reflected light in equal measure.

"Evie!" Hesta cried out, and rushed to her side.

Evie held up a hand. "Don't. Don't touch. I'm full."

"Purge," Hesta urged.

Evie looked up, her face contorted in pain and misery. "I can't."

Before them, the man screamed in rage. "Bitch! What have you done?"

Hesta stood up. "She has saved you from that curse. You're free of it. You get to live normally once more."

"Stupid cow. This was a gift to me."

"What?"

He sniffed the air. "I can still smell you. You're the Bethwood bitch."

"What? Yes. I'm Hesta Bethwood. Who are you?"

"Your death is who I am, and then I will get my reward."

Hesta started to sing.

"No, Hesta," Evie said, and she turned to the man. "Do you want the beast back?"

He stopped advancing on Hesta and turned to Evie instead. "You will give it back." It wasn't a question or a request.

"Yes," Evie said.

He smiled.

"Come here, then. I'm hurt and can't walk."

The moment he approached, Evie pressed both of her hands against his chest. Nothing happened for a long moment, but then Evie's hands turned purple. The darkness gathered around her body and shot down her arms in lines of pulsing blackness.

Evie gritted her teeth and moaned in pain. Ice covered her hair and face and chased the blackness away.

"Mine," he said.

"All of it," Evie said.

"Yes, mine."

Evie grinned. "If that's what you want, take it. Take it all."

The darkness clung to her skin like an oily film. Flakes of ice covered her pale hair and her clothing. Glowing darkly and covered in frost, Evie barely looked human.

The man howled as hair sprouted along his shoulders and over his belly. "My gift!"

His jaw elongated. His teeth grew longer and larger, and then grew straight out the sides of his face. The skin around his jaw bubbled, as though something fought to get out, and then split open. Blood dripped down his chin and splattered over his chest.

Ripples rolled over his body in waves. Muscles grew in his arms and then receded. Over and over, he was exposed to a rapid ebb and flow of change. His limbs stretched and grew, then shrank back in a rapid and unpleasant cycle. Hair grew long and coarse, then retreated into his body.

He shrieked in pain. "Stop!"

The skin over his shoulder split and a bone extended out. His knee cracked as one thigh grew longer and more substantial.

"What are you doing?" One hand deformed, part remained human while the palm became more beastly. The skin over his wrist split as though the beast needed to burst out of the human body.

'*Nearly,*' Evie said into Hesta's mind.

The blackness rolled over Evie in one final wave and gathered in her hands. "All yours!" she screamed.

He fell to his deformed knees. The indelicate aroma of old and rancid meat wafted up on a cold wave, as though the door to a butcher's frozen storage had opened.

The man fell to his side, lifeless.

"Is he?" Hesta asked.

Evie pressed two fingers to his throat. "Yeah, I think so."

"Good."

Evie wiped her hands on her skirts and drew her shoulders back. "As we were told. Someone needed to die today, and I would not let it be you, Hesta, no matter how much you crave to save me." She held out her hand to Hesta. "I'm safe now, and so are you."

"Let me look at you." More than anything, Hesta needed to see the damage to Evie's side, only barely hidden by the ragged, bloody cotton top.

"Not as bad as you think," Evie said as she exposed her wounds.

Her ribs were bruised, but the marks already looked a day or two old. Three gashes ran scored her flesh, but they were already healing, and the flow of blood had stopped.

"You look in very good condition considering a moment ago I thought you were dead."

"I thought I was a goner, too. But I don't think it was as bad as it seemed.

"Does it hurt?"

"Hell, yes," Evie said. "But at first, it was the shock that took my breath away."

Hesta put her arm around Evie's waist and helped her walk. "We'd better get help now. How on earth are we going to explain this?"

Evie shrugged. "Never mind. I'm exhausted and starving. Let's go home."

"Which home would that be?"

"Well, I think that would be the one with the salve you use when I get hurt."

Hesta couldn't stop the grin that split her face. "Bethwood House it is. It's a long walk."

Evie cocked her head to one side. "Isn't that the sound of a horse and carriage?"

Hesta strained her ears and picked up the familiar rattle. "I think it must be Charlie, coming to fetch us."

"Good. Then we can wait for an inspector to call. Again."

"He'll think this is getting to be a habit. What shall we tell him this time?" Hesta asked.

"We'll think of something on the way home."

28

They heard the shrill cry of distant whistles as Charlie drove them through Ardmore to Cainstown. They passed few people on the street until they came to the river, and then the presence of both police and civilians grew more frequent.

As they approached Salverton, they were flagged down by a small group of men. Most were of the type to enjoy a cross-city manhunt, but they had with them several members of the constabulary. Evie counted four constables and an inspector, and she groaned when she recognised Inspector Willis. "It had to be him, didn't it."

"Good morning, ladies," he said. "You are aware of the lateness of the hour?"

"We are aware of the hour, Inspector," Hesta said.

Evie tried to hide the injuries to her side, but she wasn't fast enough.

"I see you have encountered something or someone unpleasant. Do you require medical attention?"

"No, I'm fine," Evie replied.

"In that case, would you care to explain why you are here? That would make this policeman's job a simpler one."

Evie sighed. "You wouldn't believe us, even if we tried to explain."

"Try me."

"I'll start by telling you there is a dead man further down this street," Hesta said.

"Did you check for life?" he asked.

"Yes, of course. That's how I know he's dead."

The inspector nodded. "Why didn't you wait until assistance came?"

"We'd had enough waiting and were going to get help."

"And you were just being nosy about the scene here?"

"Yes," Evie answered.

He stared at them for a moment, then spoke to Charlie. "And what did you see?"

"Nothing," Charlie said. "I had a problem with ole Bess here. She were such a problem, I had to drop the ladies off for a moment before the calash overturned. I drove off to calm her down. When I came back, it were all done and a man, all naked, lay in the street. I thought it best to take the ladies home now that Bess was happy again."

"I see," Willis said. "Well, let's go back and see this man, shall we? And ladies, I would like—no, I insist, that you accompany me."

"It's late. We're tired, and I would rather go home," Hesta said.

"And I would rather have the truth from you. Unless you prefer I place you under arrest."

Hesta glared at him. "Very well. Charlie, turn us around and take us back to where you picked us up."

"Right you are, miss."

"Would you care to ride with us, Inspector? Or are you afraid we might commit some atrocity upon your good self?"

He tipped his hat to her. "How very civil of you. I'll accept the ride with you." He remained by the side of the carriage and gestured to one of the constables. "Set a guard around each of the crime scenes, then send the rest of the chaps our way."

"Yes, sir," the constable replied.

"And remind those that follow not to dawdle."

"Sir!"

As he entered the calash, the two women scrunched together to give him room. It was not a carriage meant for three.

"Off we go, Charlie," Hesta said.

Evie ignored the inspector. No matter what she'd said earlier, her whole body ached where she'd been raked by the beast's claws. She could hide the blood under what remained of her clothing, but she needed to rest. Her joints and muscles stiffened the longer they stayed in the carriage. Something else nagged at her, too. Something didn't feel right, but it was hard to think when everything hurt.

The beast had been far easier to kill than expected, for a start. She'd expected a greater challenge to her gift. Yes, Hesta had strengthened her, but without touching. And she had syphoned without touch. It was strange. Why had it been so easy?

'Evie, are you listening?' Hesta asked.

Evie had been so wrapped up in her thoughts, she hadn't realised anyone had spoken. "What?" she asked aloud.

"Are you all right?" Hesta asked. "We were talking, but you seemed off in a world of your own."

"Sorry, I was thinking things over. I'm too tired to think straight at the moment, though."

"I'll try not to keep you any longer than needed," Willis said. "Of course, it would be over much faster if you two were to tell me everything."

"Of course, Inspector," Hesta said.

Evie snorted. "So if I said there was a shapeshifting wolfman terrorizing the city, you would believe me?"

"Now then, Miss Chester, if you were on the stage, I

would howl with laughter at such comedic statements. But this is no stage, and I have no patience for frivolity."

"I don't wish to burst your bubble of innocence," Hesta said, "but there are many strange things in Bristelle. Gifted people with skills, for a start. And if there are gifted, then there are cursed, too."

Willis looked away, as though to admire the great architecture of the houses they passed. "Rumours are one thing. Truth is what I must see with my own eyes."

"Almost there," Charlie said. "I'll pull over to the side."

Evie didn't want to get out of the carriage, but Willis had no problem exiting. Hesta followed him, and Evie had to go where Hesta went.

Willis stopped in the middle of the road and stared at the remains. "You failed to mention he was undressed."

"Well, yes, because—"

"Don't tell me," he interrupted. "He was a wolfman, and when you killed him, he reverted to his true form?"

"You tell me," Hesta said.

"You wanted to see the truth with your own eyes, so you will judge things accordingly," Evie added.

Willis approached the body and turned it over. "There's not a scratch on him. Well, an old one, but that has healed."

"Did you think we knifed him or something?" Evie asked. Tiredness did not improve her mood, nor the sharpness of her tongue.

"Do you know this man?" he asked.

"No," she answered.

"Miss Bethwood?"

"No," Hesta replied.

"It seems to be a growing habit, finding dead men in your presence with no apparent cause. I must worry about you two, I think."

"Worry all you like," Evie said, "but it will just give you an acid stomach."

Willis scowled as he looked at the hands and feet of the corpse. He stared at the hands. "Miss Chester, if I were to hazard a guess as to whose blood this is, would I find it to be yours?" he asked.

Evie didn't answer.

He gestured towards her side and ribs. "Did he do that?"

"What do you think?" Evie asked.

"Might I take a look at the injury?" he asked.

Evie shrugged and lifted her arm so the tatters of her clothing hung out of the way.

Willis winced. "That must hurt."

"Yes, that's why I want to go home." Evie stated flatly.

He ripped a piece of paper from his notebook and held it against the wound on her ribs. "Hmm," he said thoughtfully. Then he held out the bloody fingers and compared them with the paper. "I see," he said. "When we started this man-hunt, we all thought it would be a straightforward thing. But when you two get involved, it seems to be anything but."

"Something is not right," Evie said. She didn't know what, her thoughts were too slow and sluggish to think deeply about any more problems.

"You are quite correct, Miss Chester. Something isn't right at all," Willis said.

The sound of running feet alerted them to the arrival of the constables. "Isolate the area," Willis said, "and wait for the wagons. Doctor Montgomery will be responsible for the discovery of anything pertinent." He pointed along the street, and a big black-covered cart drawn by four mismatched horses clattered along the road. Behind the cart marched several constables, and Evie recognised several of them.

When the wagon stopped, Joym Montgomery jumped out of the back. He wore an off-white apron that needed to be washed.

"Ahh, Inspector, here you are. And what a surprise, Evie Chester and Miss Bethwood."

"What have you got for me?" Willis asked.

"Nothing of any consequence. However, I think that the Chester-Bethwood alliance has discovered as much as I have."

Willis glared at the two women. "Indeed. They have this unfailing ability to be in the wrong place at the wrong time."

"Or the right place," Evie countered. "And maybe there would be fewer of them if people listened to us."

Willis turned away from them. "Doctor, give me something I can work with."

Joym took an envelope from his pocket and handed it to the inspector. "Evidence from one of the scenes," he said, then looked at Evie. "There are at least two bodies, and they didn't die at the same time."

"You know this how?" Willis asked.

"There are several stages to death. One of them is the pooling of blood that creates lividity of the tissue. Two different stages of lividity, two different bodies, two different times of death." He grinned. "But I know this because Miss Chester, who has helped me in the hospital morgue, is a competent assistant."

Willis stopped to look at Evie. "Is that right? Why didn't you say?"

"I think we must have," Hesta said.

Willis grunted and started to open the envelope.

"Take care, Inspector, there is not much there, and it would be easily lost," Joym said.

Willis stopped. "What's here? The salient points, please."

"Hair found on one of the bodies," Joym answered

"Hair?"

"Indeed. I'll look more closely when I get the sample back to the laboratory, but my first thought is that it's not human."

"Animal?"

"Presumably, yes," Joym agreed.

Willis nodded. "In that case, add this body to the wagon

and tell me what you can about it. There is more to see further along."

"I think now would be a good time to clear the streets rather than do much in the way of examination," Joym said. "Give me a couple of days." Then he turned to Evie. "What do you think, Miss Chester. Have you seen this body?"

"This one is safe. The ones in the wagon are safe. But I don't know about the others further up the road."

"You've been hurt," he said. "Forgive me for not noticing sooner."

"I'm fine," she answered, and waved him off.

He came to her side anyway and pushed the remains of her shirt aside to look at the damage to her ribs.

"Is everyone just going to help themselves?" Evie asked. "Enough is enough."

"Beg pardon," Joym said. "Well, it looks like you were only just raked with the fingertips. If he'd scraped harder or with a wider spread of his…" He held his hands up to demonstrate his meaning.

"Bugger," Evie said under her breath. "That's what's bothering me."

"What is?" Joym asked.

"This one has smaller hands than the one we saw before."

"Smaller hands?" Willis asked.

"Oh, right," Joym said.

Evie turned to Hesta. "Hesta, it isn't him. This wasn't the butcher after all. More like his assistant." She felt her knees start to buckle, but Joym caught her arm.

"You need to go home and get some rest," he said.

"I'll escort you both, in case someone feels like talking," Willis said.

"If you like," Hesta said. *'Are you all right?'* she asked Evie. *'Tired. But Hesta, this is the baby. There's a bigger one to catch!'*

"Go home, ladies," Joym said. "There's time for more tomorrow. Or rather, later."

29

Compared to the amount of time they'd spent racing around the city, the trip home was much shorter. Even so, Evie couldn't keep her eyes open. She leaned against Hesta's shoulder and started to drift to sleep. All too soon, she came to with a start.

"It's all right. We're almost back at the house," Hesta said.

Evie yawned and stretched. "It's been a long and tiring day." She stopped mid-stretch. "Almost?"

"It seems there is a young man, who should be home abed at this hour, who has flagged us down a little short of our destination," Willis said. "I'll give him a ticking off, shall I?"

"You'll do no such thing," Hesta said, her tone harsh and pointed. "He's a friend of mine, and you will extend him the courtesy of good manners."

"What?" Willis asked.

"Nothing. In fact, stay here," Hesta said, and she alighted from the carriage. "Evie?"

"Coming." Evie stretched one last time, then she, too, left the carriage.

The boy, slouched against the wall and half hidden in the

shadows, beckoned them over. "Got a message from Finn," he said.

This was not a boy she had seen before, but that didn't matter; he had the look of a beggar boy. "There was something, a murderous something, on the streets tonight. Are the boys all safe?" Evie asked.

He stared at her. "As if you care."

"We do, actually," Hesta said. "You can tell Finn that Sparky was right about what he saw."

He chewed on his words for a moment and chinned towards the calash. "What's 'e doin' in your carriage?"

"The inspector has escorted us home," Evie said.

"He half thinks we're the ones killing people," Hesta added.

The boy laughed. "Got ya."

"You have a message from Finn," Hesta prompted the boy.

"Yeah, he says to tell you that something is com—"

Bess threw her head in the air and snorted loudly enough to interrupt the conversation.

Charlie stood on the footboards and fought with the mare's reins. "Something's spooking her," he said. She tried to jump out of her harness and stamped her feet. "Miss, it's starting again."

Hesta grabbed the boy's arm. "Get in the carriage and get out of here."

"Inspector, get out of here with—" Evie started, but Willis had already jumped out.

"Charlie, get yourself, Bess, and the boy to safety."

The boy hardly got a chance to get in the carriage before they clattered off at an unseemly pace down the road, their haste probably not instigated by Charlie.

"Miss Bethwood, care to explain?" Willis asked.

Evie sniffed the air as though her sense of smell could give her a clue. It didn't. "Let's head to the house, shall we? The river is a bit stinky right now."

From the lane down the road, a dark shape detached itself from the shadows and lumbered into the street, much like the earlier beast, but this one was definitely larger. Taller, wider, more muscular, and bulkier. Shaggy fur covered its entire body, although the hair on its front seemed shorter and less dense. Its claws were each as long as Evie's hands and curved like scythes. The yellowed fangs, as wide as a fist, tapered into wicked points.

Unnatural blue eyes stared at them with barely a blink. It stretched its snout forward and sniffed, then it lumbered towards them on huge claw-tipped paws, the form of the leg more canine than human.

"What on this good earth is that?" Willis asked.

"The Butcher," Hesta answered. "Step away, but move slowly. Very, very slowly."

"I will need your song," Evie said. She did not have time for subtlety, and only when she had spoken out aloud did she remember she could have spoken to Hesta's mind and the inspector wouldn't have heard. *'Are you all right?'* she asked.

'Terrified,' Hesta replied.

The beast stepped forward; its long claws scraped against the cobbles of the road with a rasp like a knife grinding against sharpening steel.

"Stand back. Let this creature focus on me, not you," Evie said.

"Evie," Hesta said. Before Evie could respond, she planted a kiss on her lips. "You'll need it."

Evie smirked. She stood before a beast, success not guaranteed, and she couldn't stop herself from smiling.

Hesta blew a kiss at Willis. "And you too have my blessing," she said. "Now, get on with you."

Willis looked confused rather than scared. The beast was

neither. It approached slowly and sniffed every couple of steps, as though it wondered why they didn't run.

Evie rolled her shoulders and focused on calling her gift. Exhausted though she was, she didn't have time to allow her frailties to stop her. She pushed her gift forward, and the whole creature glittered darkly, but with a hint of blue, an unnatural blue, like its eyes.

Willis stared at the monster.

"Ready?" Evie said. She took a step forward as her gift sampled the curse. The taste of meat filled her mouth. Strong meat, rather gamey, she thought.

Evie's movement seemed to stir Willis into action. He pulled out a pistol from a place inside his jacket. "Halt!" he shouted. "Should I warn it? Does it even understand Anglish?"

"No idea," Evie said. She moved closer to the creature. '*If I fall, run,*' she said to Hesta's mind.

'*You will not fall.*' Hesta replied.

She tried to call the darkness, but it would not come to her. She would have to touch it, then, and she hoped she could absorb the curse fast enough that she could send it back before she died.

The creature cocked its head to one side, its ears pointed forwards as though concerned or at least interested in this little creature that approached. It folded over to stand on all fours and stared at Evie as it raised a taloned hand and drew its claws over the stones.

"I know what you are," Evie said.

The beast stopped and sniffed the air. Its huge head swung from her to Hesta. A long red tongue rasped over its muzzle and between its teeth.

"Come closer and you can get a better sense of who I am," Evie said.

Its attention refocused on Evie.

'*Now,*' she said directly to Hesta's mind.

Hesta's gift hit her ears with the screeching of metal against metal. It shuddered through her and pierced her insides.

And then it didn't.

Instead, Hesta's song flowed with her and through her. Strength filled every bone within her body and she felt…she felt invincible. When she called to the darkness, it responded without delay. With it, the curse brought a great wave of aromatics. The stench of burning rotten meat filled her nose and her mouth with vileness. Evie almost gagged, but Hesta's song supported her so she could ignore the revolting taste in her mouth, even when the flavour slipped down her throat and settled like a block of hot acid in her belly.

The beast yelped at their joined attack, and it hunched down ready to spring. It seemed uncertain and sluggish. The smaller one had moved with greater certainty and speed than this one. Evie marked the difference as an oddity to consider later.

"What on this good earth is that noise?" Willis said.

"Shut up. You have a gun; use it or go away," Evie said.

Willis moved to her side. He raised the gun and shot the beast in the face. It whimpered, and a huge clawed hand swiped at its snout. Blood seeped down the creature's muzzle and matted the shaggy hair under its chin in red-tipped peaks.

Willis shot again, this time into the creature's broad and muscular chest. Not just once. He fired shot after shot until the gun clicked empty.

The beast roared in pain and defiance and focused its attention on Willis. It tried to leap but stumbled before it could find traction. Instead, it rose in a languid flow to stand upright and stepped closer the source of its pain.

Willis released the clip on the empty magazine and it dropped into his hand. With practiced ease he changed the magazine and clipped a new one into his gun. He moved with such calm sureness that it was hard to believe he stood off with a seven-foot monster. He aimed once more and fired.

A rage filled roar filled the air as the creature targeted Willis. It no longer paid Evie or Hesta any attention. He grabbed the inspector's face in one giant hand and dragged the man closer.

Evie couldn't have that. Willis would not survive that kind of contact without help. She focused her attention on the sense of darkness glittering within the beast—the primary source of the infection.

"I see you," she yelled. "Come to me."

'*Evie?*' echoed inside her mind.

"Sing, Hesta, sing for me," Evie yelled. '*I can see the darkness. Sing me your strength and the song that helps me, the one I think of as the song of calling.*'

As soon as Hesta's gift-filled voice rose in song, Evie began to syphon the blackness from the beast. It paused then, its teeth no more than an inch away from biting into Willis.

The beast turned its shaggy head to her and threw Willis to the ground. Although Evie didn't know if he was alive, she didn't have time to think about him anymore.

A single gunshot made Evie jump. The beast growled and shook its head as a spot of blood seeped from the edge of its neck.

More shots followed, and with each one, Evie shuddered with pain.

Pain and rage. The *beast's* pain and rage.

Yet she did not stop syphoning. Her hands turned black with scintillating bursts of bright blue.

'*Faster. More,*' Evie sent.

Hesta's song changed. For a moment, it became light and energetic. The speed at which the curse was drawn into Evie increased to almost unbearable levels.

Icy blue flames rolled over her hands, over her arms, and across her shoulders until the cold fire consumed her and she glowed with a flickering blue light. She held her arms to the side as the curse turned her into a living pyre.

Almost unbearable pain ripped through Evie's body, but she couldn't cry out. The flames turned her clothing to ash, charred her skin, and seared through to the bone. Yet her gift would not let her go, and it wouldn't let her die in peace.

The beast roared and turned its attention from Willis to her. With one limping bound, the creature landed before her and swept her up. It screamed as her flames jumped from her to it, and it dropped her onto the cobbled street. As Evie fell to her knees, it clawed at her with talons long and sharp. One pierced her shoulder as the creature slammed her to the ground and pinned her down.

The pain grew, yet still she drew the darkness into her. She no longer needed to call the curse; her gift pulled at it all on its own.

The beast roared into her face and prepared to sink its long, pointed teeth into her neck. It paused, sniffed her, and then licked along the length of her cheek.

Evie tried to struggle, but there was little she could do. The creature weight pinned her down and almost crushed her.

She saw Hesta at her side. She still raised her voice in song, but it was a soothing melody now, as though to keep Evie's pain at bay.

In the absence of a weapon, Hesta shoulder-charged the limb that held Evie to the ground. It didn't do anything, but she'd tried, and she didn't stop trying.

Brave Hesta.

Evie felt a sharp stabbing sensation in her thigh. She tried to scream, but her cry died on her lips and she whimpered instead.

The beast screamed and backed away. It held a rear paw in the air. Sticking out of its leg, a knife hilt glittered in the blue light. The creature limped back, panting, its head low slung.

Willis grabbed the hilt of the knife and twisted it inside the beast's leg.

For a moment Evie's pain grew so great, she thought she would die of it. She drew one long ragged breath and waited for the agony to subside, or at least until she could live with it.

"Give up the beast, whoever you are. Let it go," she croaked, her voice hoarse.

The beast started to transform. Hair dropped from its skin, and the shorter hair receded. Normal, human skin could be seen underneath. Bullet holes oozed blood that ran down its chest. It stood up and bellowed. Evie could hear the rage in its voice, and the bullets pushed out of its skin and fell to the ground. The skin started to close as the shots fell away.

"It takes more than that," the beast grumbled, a distinctly male voice. His words were slurred together, and he spoke with a mouth that contained far too many teeth, making him hard to understand.

"I will heal," he said, and he stood there, more man than beast. Although the beastly parts, such as his claws and teeth, made him look just as monstrous for having so many human features.

"No, you won't," Evie said.

He sank to his knees and groaned. "What have you done to me?"

She held her glowing hands in front of her. "I have stolen your powers."

He shook his head. "I can still feel it."

"But it is weak," Evie said.

Willis approached the man but didn't get too close. The inspector, it seemed, was a smart man. Gashes across his head and face oozed with blood; this beast had done him a great deal of hurt. He gulped at the air and asked, "Who the hell are you? *What* are you?"

The beast cocked his head to one side, and for a moment

the unnatural blue returned to his eyes with great strength. "Police?" He laughed. "You had no idea, did'ya?"

"How many did you make?" Evie asked.

He looked surprised at the question. "You guessed?"

"The other was lesser," Evie admitted.

"Children," said the beast, "are often a disappointment."

"How many children?" Hesta asked.

He grinned—or grimaced, it was hard to tell. "You tell me."

Willis stood upright; he still breathed heavily, but less so. "Why, man? Why?"

The beast glared at him.

"You're not a shifter, and not a werewolf either. Those are gifts, not a curse," Hesta said. "Once upon a time, they would have called you a lycanthrope. A cursed wolfman."

He shrugged, and as he moved, his claws grated across the stones of the roadway. "Clever Bethwood."

"Why are you here?" Evie asked.

The beast grinned and eased himself to his knees. He pulled the knife from his thigh, and at first the blood oozed out. Then it stopped.

"Stay where you are!" Willis yelled.

"Or you'll do what?" the beast asked. "Take me into custody?"

Willis didn't answer.

"I come for the slave."

"Which one?" Evie asked.

He lurched towards Hesta. Hair sprouted along his arms. Evie stepped forward and intercepted his approach. Her glowing hands turned into hands holding a sickly blue flame.

"Sing for me," Evie shouted. '*Sing and let's gift him all that I have of him.*'

It took a moment for Hesta to find her voice, but when she did sing, it was as though she stood inches away instead of a few feet. So much power came from her that although Evie couldn't absorb all of the curse, she gathered her flame and all she had already absorbed and threw it back at the creature in one great wave of her gift.

The blue flames burst into light, and as Evie reached out to him, the flames jumped from her to him. She returned his curse, and when the blue flame died, the chill of the void roared up and turned the fire purple. She threw that at him as well. With Hesta's strength, she returned all she had syphoned as fast as she could. She knew what would happen once she finished. In her mind's eye, she saw the shocked face of Eric, the first man she had killed with her gift.

The beast man screamed in agony and frustration. He started to transform, but so fast he blurred in front of her eyes.

"No," he murmured. Then he whispered, "The siren will die." He fell to the ground and lay still, a man, and no more than that.

Evie stepped back and fell against Hesta.

"I have you," Hesta said.

"Shoot him," Evie said.

"No need," Willis said. He knelt at the man's side and tested his pulse. "He's dead. Would you care to tell me what the hell just happened?"

"You saw," Hesta said.

"Yes, and I don't believe my own eyes," he replied.

"Well, you saw this one. Get him collected, and I'll get Evie inside. She needs to have her injuries seen to." She didn't wait for a reply but led Evie into the house.

"I think you need to have your injuries treated as well, Inspector," Evie said over her shoulder.

"Am I infected?" he asked.

Evie looked and shook her head. "Not that I can see."

30

E vie sat at the kitchen table and nibbled on a sweet
biscuit. Hesta bathed her wounds in heated water, and
she had a fair few of them to bathe. There were the remnants
of the raking across her ribs and a deep puncture wound to
her shoulder. Numerous burn marks covered her back, arms,
and neck. There were probably more that she hadn't even
considered yet. She felt enough pain without trying to
catalogue each one.

"I really don't know how you can sit upright right now,"
Hesta said.

"Nor me. I'm exhausted. And I'm hungry." Evie finished
her biscuit and yawned. "Do you think I could get dressed
sometime soon? The heat from the stove is nice, but, well, I'm
cold." She pulled the blanket around her waist and shifted
until it draped over the undamaged shoulder.

"Shush and be still. I can't get this done if you fidget so."

"I'm fine. There's no need for this. I'm not going to get
infected."

"Be patient. There is every need to make sure you're all
right. I'll make tea as soon as I know for sure." She used the

heated water and a clean piece of linen as she moved to the next open gash.

It was nice to be cared for. And even though it hurt when Hesta touched her ribs, she merely hissed at the discomfort. The shoulder wound hurt a lot more.

"It's still bleeding. Shall I stitch it?"

Evie stared at the hole for a moment. "No. Just cover it with a wad of clean cotton, or linen, and wrap it."

"I'd like to use some iodine on this, but I don't have any. Nor do I have any herbs. I should know by now that with you around, I'm going to need to invest in a first aid kit."

Evie chuckled, but it hurt. "A little of that salve will do."

"Will it?"

"Well, you put it on so nicely, how could I not ask for more?" Evie asked. Hesta stared at her, and Evie swore she could see tears.

Hesta turned her attention to the many burns that covered Evie's skin. They were not red, as if from scalding hot water, nor blistered. Instead, it looked as though her skin had been burned off in some places. She put a finger under Evie's chin so she could see the scorch marks that covered her neck and throat.

"What about these burns? How are you not writhing in pain?"

"Touch one," Evie instructed.

Hesta shook her head. "No."

Evie grabbed her hand and placed it on a burn that covered the top of her knee.

"It'll hurt if I tou—" Her words stopped dead. "Cold?"

"When I started to burn, the cold came to me. And yes, if you are wondering, it hurts."

"Will salve help?"

Evie looked into her eyes. "Yes."

Hesta put a little onto her fingertips and smoothed the ointment to the burns on Evie's face and neck. To Evie, it felt an intimate moment. Hesta cared about her, and she applied herself so carefully to the task that Evie closed her eyes and let the salve and Hesta's gentle touch soothe her battered skin.

Hesta had almost finished spreading the salve when a loud and resolute knock at the front door disturbed them.

"Three guesses?" Hesta asked.

"If it's the inspector, let him in, I suppose. I just need something to wear. You do know I have no more spare clothing?"

"I know." Hesta grabbed a tunic and a robe from the back of the door. "I got these from the laundry. It's better than a sheet."

"Shall we go to the drawing room to meet him?"

"No. Stay here. I'll bring him in, and if he wants to ask more silly questions, he can do so here."

"It would be nice if we could be alone for a while and talk this through. Such a lot has happened."

"I know, so would I, but I don't think we'll be allowed yet."

Evie sighed. "I know."

Hesta left her alone for a few moments and went to the front door. Mrs Dunn would be still be abed, but it wouldn't be long before she rose. Charlie had not long returned from calming Bess. No one would be getting much rest tonight. Or this morning.

"How are you, Miss Chester?" Willis asked as he came into the kitchen. "I have a great many questions for you both."

"I thought you might," Evie said.

"I'd better make some tea then, eh?" Hesta said.

Willis stood near the kitchen door, his hands behind his back as he rocked on the balls of his feet. He'd wiped his cuts, but dried blood clung to his hair and down the side of his neck.

"Relax," Hesta said. "Take a seat if you will."

"I'm fine here," he replied.

"As you will," Hesta said as she prepared the tea.

"Are you here to question us?" Evie asked. She winced as she turned to face him.

Willis looked uncomfortable at the sight of her. "You look unwell."

"Unwell? I've been scorched to a crisp. Now, get on with your questions."

"I have many, but right now, I wanted to ask a couple of things in particular," he said.

Hesta handed Evie a strong cup of tea and added several spoonfuls of sugar.

"What do you need then?" Evie asked.

"What the hell was that?"

"What it was is a complex question, but the gist of it is that he is, or was, a lycanthrope," Hesta said.

"You said that outside, but I don't know what that is."

"A cursed wolfman," Hesta said.

"A werewolf?"

"Of a sort."

"And what are you?" he asked.

Evie grinned. "That's an easy one. We're gifted, Inspector. Plain and simple."

"That's not enough. I need to know more," he said.

"When we know that we are safe from you, we'll tell you more," Evie said.

"Of course you are safe from me. But what do I put in the report? I need you to trust me," he said.

Evie nodded at that. "Fair enough, but right now, I only trust you enough to speak with you about what happened this evening, but no more. I cannot share what might come back to haunt me."

"So you would rather be a suspect for murder than allow people to know you are gifted?"

"Rumours will follow us anyway. It is better to be a suspect than let fear and superstitions find us guilty without trial."

He considered that as Hesta handed him a cup of tea. He refused the milk and sugar and stared into the depths of his cup before he could summon words.

"Is what happened to the man outside the same thing that happened to your brother and Mister Halms?" He looked most uncomfortable with the question.

"No," Hesta said. "Ekvard Halms had been possessed by a demon that infected my brother. The demon had attempted to infect others. We suspect it wished to take over and control the whole city. It killed my brother out of spite because we thwarted its plans."

"Oh, Great Mother, have mercy on our souls," he said. "What other beasts are out there stalking the streets of Bristelle?"

"That's a very good question," Hesta said. "There are and will be others."

"What the hell do we do about it?" he asked.

"You must let us do what we can. Fewer people will die that way," Hesta said. "Now you see the need for an academy. A safe place for the gifted to live and learn."

He nodded.

"Never mind that. Now that the beast is dead, what are you going to do about us?" Evie asked.

"Nothing. I'm going to go now so you can get some rest and mend yourself. When you have recovered, come and see me. I need to make sure that the official report mirrors what you saw. Speak only to me, however."

"Maybe you should make your notes here rather than at the station?" Hesta asked.

He considered her point. "Yes. Good idea. After that, I'm sure there are times when I shall value your help and your expertise. This is not the first time something unnatural has happened in the city."

"It won't be the last, either," Evie said.

"No," he said. "I can't say that it will. If I need help, can I ask for your assistance?"

"Yes, of course you can," Evie replied. "If you help us in return."

"Then I look forward to working with you again." He stared at the floor for a moment. "Is the beast really dead?"

"Yes," Hesta answered.

"But if I were you, I'd ask Doctor Montgomery to cremate the remains as soon as he can. Just in case," Evie said.

Willis nodded. "I'll do that. Straight away." He didn't make any move to leave, though. "Miss Chester."

"Yes?"

He gestured to his face. "Will you be all right?"

She smiled. "I'll be as right as rain in a few days or weeks. Miss Bethwood has a large jar of herbal salve that works wonders."

"Good. Very good." He nodded. "Well, I shall bid you both a good night. I will let myself out." With that, he left them in the kitchen.

Neither spoke until they heard the front door close with a solid *thunk*.

"That will be helpful," Evie said.

"At least he's stopped trying to pin the murders on us."

"This could be very promising for the academy, as well as for us."

Hesta nodded. "*Was* the beast really dead?"

"As much as I can tell, but burning it will make certain."

"And how about you? Can you use your skills and purge?"

"We'll know as soon as I can find someone to practice on. But not for a while yet. I think we deserve a few restful days."

"Until the next time."

I hope you have enjoyed this story. If you did, please consider leaving an honest review. Most of all, I just want to know that you have enjoyed the story.

Thank you

If you want to know more about new books, background details and information not printed any place else, then subscribe to the reader's list.

https://www.subscribepage.com/nitaround

Visit my website at
www.nitaround.com

Or join my facebook group

www.facebook.com/groups/nitaroundbooks/

More Books in the Towers world

The Towers of the Earth

Prequel: A Pinch of Salt
Prequel: A Hint of Hope
Book 1: A Touch of Truth
Book 2: A Touch of Rage
Book 3: A Touch of Darkness
Book 4: A Touch of Ice

The Evie Chester Files:

Case 1: Lost and Found
Case 2: Sirens and Syphons
Case 3: Fur and Fangs

Printed in Great Britain
by Amazon